NOT INTO TEMPTATION

Rejected by local landowner Sir George Foxcroft, Hannah Brockley opens a girls' school in the family home to achieve financial security for herself and her sister Margaret. But then one of the older pupils dies in suspicious circumstances. Both the sympathetic Reverend William Woodward and the handsome Dr Shipley were present that night. Will they help Hannah through a perilous spiral of danger and deceit to find the happiness she seeks — or could one of them be implicated in the crime?

Books by Anne Hewland
in the Linford Romance Library:

STOLEN SECRET
TO TRUST A STRANGER
A SUBTLE DECEIT
BLIGHTED INHERITANCE
A DANGEROUS REFUGE
DREAM OF DANGER
POOL OF DARKNESS
THE FATAL FLAW
HANDLE WITH CARE

ANNE HEWLAND

NOT INTO TEMPTATION

Complete and Unabridged

LINFORD
Leicester

First published in Great Britain in 2016

First Linford Edition
published 2018

*A catalogue record for this book is available
from the British Library.*

ISBN 978–1–4448–3578–6

Published by
F. A. Thorpe (Publishing)
Anstey, Leicestershire

Set by Words & Graphics Ltd.
Anstey, Leicestershire
Printed and bound in Great Britain by
T. J. International Ltd., Padstow, Cornwall
This book is printed on acid-free paper

Prologue

Hannah stared out of the drawing-room window into the grey November day. It had been almost a year now since their father had died; surely Sir George must speak soon? If she stood on her toes, she could see the tips of the chimneys of Hartstock Hall, across their grounds and his. Even if they could only have a quiet ceremony, he must soon fulfil dear Father's hopes, as he had promised. And he had been so helpful. He must realise how difficult life had become now for Hannah and Margaret.

Margaret burst into the room. Hannah turned, the words *quietly now*, frozen on her lips as she saw the look on her sister's face.

'Oh, Hannah! I have been talking to Mrs Copley in the kitchen. They are saying in the village that Sir George is married!'

Hannah swayed, staying upright only by an effort of will as she felt the blood drain from her face. As if someone else was speaking, she heard the broken phrases, 'Idle gossip. Cannot be true.'

'It *is* true. He has brought her home. Mrs Copley's sister has seen her.'

Hannah was shaking her head. 'No, no.' She straightened, knowing what she must do. 'I shall go and ask him. He cannot know what is being said.'

'I'll come too.'

'No, thank you. I need to go alone.' She did not believe it, not for one moment. When he heard of the lies that were circulating, Sir George would be shocked. It might even be a blessing in disguise, motivating him to make her the offer she craved.

Without further thought, she was in her outdoor clothes and running along the path she had taken so many times before, leaving Hartstock Grange and their own grounds behind, crossing the uneven terrain where the path traversed the rough banks of a small stream and

2

rising again to see the Hartstock Hall roof and chimneys near at hand. The hall and the grange had once belonged to one landowner, but as so often happened in families, had been split and sold.

No need to hurry on to enter the grounds of the hall, for here was Sir George coming to meet her. Her heart leapt, but she could hardly speak or catch her breath.

'Hannah, my dear!' He strolled towards her, hands outstretched. 'Whatever is the matter?' She blurted it out as he smiled. He said, 'Of course! And you are hurrying to congratulate me.'

Her eyes wide, Hannah could only say, 'It's true?'

'Indeed so. I am blessed with good fortune.'

'But my father always hoped — '

'Ah, yes. My very good friend as he was, wanting nothing but the best for you and me. But you know as well as I do that such a match would have been impossible. An estate such as mine is

3

expensive to maintain, and Hartstock Grange also. I could not follow my inclinations. I had to marry money.'

Hannah's throat felt tight. She must not betray her true feelings. She tried to be dignified. 'Then I do not see what is to become of us. How can I continue to care for Margaret?'

Sir George said kindly, 'Do not despair. I understand your problem.' He produced a piece of thin card from his pocket. 'In the absence of good fortune such as mine, and being unable to attract a wealthy husband, why not try something like this? See . . . '

She took it from him, the words blurring before her eyes. *The Misses Brontë*. She frowned. Who were they? What could he mean?

'There is little chance of this particular venture succeeding, for Haworth is far too remote — but see how conveniently placed the grange would be. And you and Margaret would have an income to solve all your problems while remaining at home. An ideal solution.'

4

She was making sense of the words now. 'A school? But who would send their daughters here?'

'Oh, I can assist you there. I can help to distribute similar prospectus cards to suitable families from Leeds to Manchester. And of course my new wife also has many useful contacts.'

'Thank you.' How she longed to throw his idea and the card back in his face. But how would that help Margaret? She could see straightaway that she must pocket her pride. With an effort, she achieved a brilliant smile. 'The very thing. What a wonderful suggestion.' While within, her heart felt as if it were breaking in two.

1

Hannah was lying awake, worrying as always about the survival of the school. Five years on, and the venture that had begun with hope and the determination to put Sir George's betrayal behind her was on the verge of failure. Perhaps her dinner party that evening would have helped in the urgent need for more pupils, as she had hoped her guests would understand and recommend her.

As the snow began to fall, Sir George and Lady Foxcroft had cried off, but the doctor and the dissenting minister were made of sterner stuff. A fierce and sudden blizzard obscuring the paths and hazards, however, had caused them both to accept her invitation to stay overnight. It was an unfortunate circumstance, but it gave Hannah further opportunities to impress, demonstrating how efficiently the school was run.

She half-smiled to herself. Yes, her little social occasion had had a serious purpose; but just for one evening it had been pleasant to share interesting male company with her sister, the sheen of their best dresses catching the candle-light. And surely Dr Shipley had regarded her approvingly? She did not think she had imagined it. A pity Lady Foxcroft had not been present after all to witness the sparkling exchanges. And if the doctor could allow his regard to become something warmer ... ? Hannah hardly dared think it.

Then came the screams piercing the night. Hannah sat upright, tense with shock. As she threw a shawl over her nightgown, she was angry. Whatever was Violet thinking of, to allow such behaviour? Had Hannah been wrong to put her in charge of a dormitory? And tonight too, with the two unexpected guests; it was of the utmost importance to impress them. Particularly the doctor.

Oh no. As she sped silently down the

corridor, their doors were opening. 'Please, do not be concerned,' she said quickly. 'It's nothing. Some of the girls are prone to nightmares.'

One door closed, but Mr Woodward, undeterred, was following. The minister murmured, 'Even so, I may be of some assistance.'

Hannah burst into the far dormitory, where it was Lavinia who was shrieking while four smaller girls, screaming and sobbing, clustered at the end of the room by the window.

'Lavinia!' Hannah cried. 'What are you doing in here?' No one heard her. She could hardly hear herself. She drew breath and raised her arms. 'Be quiet!' The noise stopped. One of the smallest was whimpering. Hannah said firmly, 'Where is Violet? She should be in charge in this room,' glancing over to Violet's bed as she spoke.

'Oh, Miss Hannah,' Lavinia moaned. 'Violet is dead!'

Hannah felt as if someone had struck her. She swayed a little. No — she must be strong. 'But yesterday she seemed perfectly well.' Of course they had been fortunate that none of the girls had suffered any serious illnesses; they had a sensible regime of learning and exercise, and a nourishing diet. But sudden death could occur anytime. She leaned over the body, seeking a pulse in the thin throat, any sign of a breath. There was a faint, slightly familiar smell that she could not immediately place.

Behind her in the corridor, the minister was calling quietly, 'Dr Shipley, we have need of you.'

Hannah took a calming breath. 'Come, girls; you must go to the other dormitory for tonight. Three to a bed if needs be. Miss Margaret will settle you.'

For here, belatedly, was Margaret, yawning and with her dark hair rumpled. Too much wine, Hannah thought, a little unkindly. No wonder her sister had not noticed Lavinia's absence. Or the noise.

'Margaret, there has been a problem

with Violet. Take the other girls back with you to your room.' She placed a reassuring hand on Lavinia's shoulder. 'I know this has been distressing for you, but you are to be calm. There is no purpose in spreading panic. I shall deal with everything now.' She frowned, observing excitement as well as distress on Lavinia's beautiful face. Hardly a suitable reaction. But Lavinia obeyed her, quietly following the others.

Here was the doctor, answering the minister's summons. He had taken the time to bring a candle, his curling hair gold in the light of the flame. Hannah regarded him with relief.

'So, Doctor, is there anything to be done?' A foolish question — obviously there was not. Hannah tried again. 'What do you consider the cause of death?'

He shrugged. 'A puerile fever, no doubt. She is — was — at a dangerous age. Young girls can suffer various noxious influences at this time of tumult.'

Hannah was disappointed at his response. 'Can you be more specific, please?' He winced and she put a weary hand to her forehead. 'I'm sorry. This has been a shock. And I am concerned for the other girls — if she should be contagious . . . '

The minister said, 'Might I make a suggestion? My friend here cannot be expected to reach a measured conclusion now. It is too dark for a thorough examination. When he can examine the poor girl in daylight, we will know more.'

'Of course.' Hannah nodded.

'Indeed, yes,' Dr Shipley said. 'We are both at your service, naturally. But there is no obvious sign of a rash or other symptoms of infection. No need for concern on that score, I am sure. And if the other girls are sleeping elsewhere, that will be a wise precaution for now. Reassurance, yes. That will be best. Apoplexy, I expect, or a weak heart. And I will view the body again in the morning.'

Hannah thought quickly. There was nothing else to be done, with the doctor already present. Impossible to notify anyone else, with the snow and the fog. The minister was right. She said, 'I will sit here with the — with Violet. She cannot be left alone. Could one of you stay with her while I reassure the other girls and Miss Margaret?'

'I will stay,' the Reverend Woodward said firmly. 'I am well accustomed to night-time vigils in my calling. And to being woken at all hours.'

Hannah nodded, whisking away to convey a steadiness she did not feel. As she had hoped, already the smaller girls were seeking consolation with arms around each other in their shared beds. Hopefully they would sleep soon.

Margaret was more of a problem. 'How like Violet!' she muttered. 'Always so dramatic. I never liked her, you know.' At least she was speaking quietly.

'That is hardly an appropriate opinion just now,' Hannah said. She looked over towards Lavinia's bed. The older girl was asleep already, or pretending to be. 'The doctor thinks Violet was not infectious and will give a more thorough opinion in the morning.' No harm in Lavinia overhearing *that* at any rate. 'Now, Margaret, I am relying upon you to maintain order and calm in here. But I will only be in the other dormitory, sitting with . . . Violet, if you should need me.' She did not mention the minister. Poor Margaret would be sure to make an inappropriate remark.

Hannah dressed swiftly, bundling her hair into a knot. But, returning, could not see him. He had already placed two stools beside Violet's bed, but both were empty. 'Mr Woodward?' she said, her voice uncertain.

'Ah, Miss Hannah.' He was standing by the furthest window, also fully dressed.

She nodded her thanks and sat down wearily. Her limbs were leaden, but the turmoil in her head was worse than ever. The death was such a shock. She felt at fault, which was ridiculous. But

14

her pupils had been entrusted to her care.

Hannah realised Mr Woodward had spoken; she nodded without having the least idea of what he had said. She stared at the girl. You could imagine her to be merely asleep. And yet something was not right.

'She looks so uncomfortable,' Hannah murmured. One arm was angled across her pillow, while her hair was disordered.

Mr Woodward said, 'Some people might sleep in such a position, I suppose.'

But not Violet. Hannah had checked the two dormitories often enough to know well how Violet had been hunched and silent in sleep. She reached out, hoping to make her seem more ordered, and then stopped, unwilling to touch her.

'Perhaps we sent the doctor away too soon,' Mr Woodward murmured. 'But she can be righted in the morning, after he has seen her again. You will need

Peggy Kershaw for the laying out; I can arrange that for you.'

'Yes. Thank you.' She must overcome her reluctance. Poor Violet. She smoothed the dark hair from the pale forehead and gasped in shock. One moment her hand seemed to be transfixed, and the next she was snatching it away as if the lifeless flesh had burned her. She stared at the minister. 'Do you see?' she whispered.

He was staring at what Hannah had unwittingly revealed: there was a large bruise on Violet's temple. 'Perhaps she fell yesterday?'

'I would have known of it. She would have complained.'

'You would think so. And see . . . ' He leaned forward also. ' . . . at the base of her throat. Are those bruises?'

'Yes,' Hannah whispered. 'But I don't understand. How could she have come by marks like that?'

Abruptly, Mr Woodward punched one palm with his other hand. Hannah jumped in shock. He said, 'I am a fool.

Will you excuse me for a few moments?'

'Why? Where are you going?'

'Do not be alarmed. I merely wish to . . . look at something.'

'By prevaricating in this way, you *are* alarming me.'

'Of course. I'm sorry. I underestimate you.' He hesitated. 'But we have all concluded Violet's death to be a natural one, as so many deaths are in the young. I now wonder if that is so.'

'What?' Hannah was staring at him in horror. 'What do you mean?'

'I feel I should examine all the doors and windows. She may have been the victim of some intruder.'

Hannah clenched her hands, resisting a wave of faintness. 'Surely that's not possible?' She could not prevent an anxious glance over her shoulder. She had been willing to keep this vigil alone. She shuddered. And yet — was the minister being too swift with his conclusions? She said only, 'Yes, a sensible idea, I suppose.'

'But I can't leave you here alone. Although after hearing the screams, any attacker must have fled. Ah, I have a better idea.'

Hannah did not like the way he was allowing his conclusions such a free rein. 'Yes?'

'I was forgetting the snowfall. With this room being at the end of the corridor and having windows on two sides, I think I am right in assuming we overlook both outer doors and many of the lower windows here?'

'Ah, I see what you mean. There would be footprints. But we can only see the front door — although the rear door is merely round the corner of the building.'

'If you look at that side, I will go here.' He was striding across the room and gesturing to her to go to the far window. Hannah found herself obeying without thinking. She was looking down over the snow-covered drive to the front door. The icy whiteness was clear and unbroken in the moonlight.

The snow had stopped, but patches of fog hung in the distant dips and hollows. She shivered, feeling as if the fog had entered the school to lurk and wisp among the rooms and corridors and would be reluctant to disperse.

But no. Be sensible. There were no footprints, no sign of anyone approaching in the last few hours. She exhaled a sigh of relief. The minister was right.

Silently, he was standing beside her. She put a hand briefly to her heart.

'I'm sorry,' he said. 'I didn't intend to startle you. Is there anything here?'

'No.'

'Then there has been no intruder. Good. The poor girl must have met with some unlucky accident.' He paused. 'All the same, I will check the ground floor if I may, to be completely certain. At least I may leave you here with Violet with a quiet mind.'

'Indeed.' Again, Hannah found herself agreeing with him. It seemed the easiest course. She sat down on her stool as he left the room, still feeling numb as she looked down at the sad figure. Not a popular girl. Not a girl it had been easy to like. *An unworthy thought*. She must regard all her pupils impartially.

With the candle now lit, it was easier to examine Violet's thin face. The blow was ugly indeed, and there was further bruising and blood in the long mouse-coloured hair. But would it have killed her? She frowned, remembering how a blow to a certain spot on the temple could indeed kill; it had happened to one of the farm workers in her childhood. His wife had come to Hannah's father in distress, but Mr Brockley had refused to help her.

'What occurred during his day's work was nothing — a mere tap. Falling down when drunk was what killed him. I cannot give recompense for his folly. You can stay in the cottage until the end of the month, and that is all I can offer.'

Hannah sighed. The woman's wails had affected her deeply as she trudged away. But why think of that now? The situation was quite different. Violet hadn't been drinking. Hannah leaned forward again. No, of course the girl did not smell of drink. She did not smell of anything at all. Not now. She must have imagined that sweetish scent.

Had the minister noticed it? And what was keeping him? Hannah stood up again, suddenly restless. Weary as she was, she could hardly sit still. She began pacing up and down the room, doubting herself. Had there truly been no prints in the snow? Supposing she had been mistaken and had unwittingly sent the minister into danger? And what about *his* side of the house, where the snow would be in the moon's shadow? No, it was all right. Her window was as she had stated. Nothing. And his?

She crossed the room and looked out to where the mist was obscuring the view over the valley; she could hardly see the edge of the drop, known locally as the Cliff, near where the house stood. She looked down into the shadows and gasped, putting a hand to her throat.

Here, the snow was not pure and untrodden. Here were the tell-tale marks, indistinct in the shadow but unmistakeable. Not an intruder, however; someone with small, light feet. Two tracks. The steps went away towards the kitchen door and were lost in the darkness of the stables, only to return. Who? Millie, perhaps, their willing little kitchen maid, slipping out to meet an admirer? It didn't seem like her. Hannah gave a soft moan, her throat cold, unwilling to contemplate what might have been going on.

Beneath her, a movement near the corner caught her eye. She stared down, pressing back against the wall by the window. The man below did not look up, although his movements were cautious. She pressed a hand to her mouth.

It was the minister, steadily destroying the prints as he brushed the snow with his feet.

2

Hannah stepped away quickly and sank down onto the stool, her legs giving way beneath her. Why was Mr Woodward concealing the footprints? She had trusted him tonight, in this difficult situation. He had taken charge; she had thankfully allowed him to do so. Had she been wrong? And what was he doing now? She could not sit here without knowing.

Cautiously she approached the window once more, standing back to avoid being seen. He had found a broken branch and was making short work of the other prints, glancing around and even upwards before disappearing from view around the corner. He must be coming back now.

What was she to say to him? Should she come straight out with what she had seen, or wait and see what he said?

She looked around Violet's, bed and there were the girl's shoes placed underneath, although not as neatly as they should have been. Hannah leaned forward and picked them up. As she had feared, they were damp. She replaced them quickly.

She still did not know what she would say when she heard Mr Woodward at the door. At least the flickering of the candle might disguise her expression — but his also. Here he was, shaking his head. She said, 'What did you find?'

He spread his hands. 'There is nothing there. All is well.'

She opened her mouth, closed it, and began again. 'If you *had* found signs of intruders, please do not spare me. I would rather know what we have to face.'

'There is no sign of any intruder, I do assure you.'

Hannah clicked her tongue, annoyed with herself. She had allowed him to answer truthfully but evasively. She had known those small prints must belong to a girl or a small woman. But had they been joined by others further along; those of a man she was to meet? And it seemed — for she must face up to this — that the woman had been Violet.

Try something else. As the minister sat down, she looked at his feet. 'Have you been out? Your shoes seem wet.' She couldn't tell, but he was not to know that.

'Ah, yes. Easier to check everything by going outside. Yes, I had a look round out there.' He turned to face her, his blue eyes intense. 'I do so admire the brave effort you have made in setting up your school. I understand how this will give your poor dear sister security and a purpose. And if there should be anything that would endanger your venture, well, please feel you can always count me your friend.'

She stared at him. 'Thank you, but why are you telling me this? We were discussing what you saw outside.'

25

'If I should ever come across anything to put your school at risk, be assured I shall take action accordingly.' He shook his head. 'I don't feel I should say anything further at present. It wouldn't help.'

Was he telling her he had destroyed the prints to protect her school and its reputation? She had no idea why he should do such a thing. If discovered, he would destroy his own reputation. Confused, she said again, 'Thank you.'

'If you wish to go and sleep for a while, I can do our duty here. We could take turn and turn about.'

'No; as I said, It is important to me that I stay.' No, indeed. She would not know what he might be doing otherwise. She would be giving him the freedom to wander around the building in the dark. What else might he discover and feel he must conceal or alter? Perhaps she was being unfair. She added, 'I am too tired to sleep, if that makes sense.'

'I understand. Naturally, I'm accustomed to missing sleep. I catch up by dozing occasionally, and in the morning feel little the worse.'

She nodded, while being determined to stay alert.

In spite of her good intentions, she found herself jerking awake — but the minister was sitting silently as if in thought or prayer. And she must have slept again, for she woke abruptly with the minister saying gently, 'Miss Brockley, the doctor is ready.'

Indeed he was, and he greeted her with an unconvincing smile.

'Good morning. I am here to fulfil my duties in daylight. You may retire now.'

Hannah brushed down her skirt as she stood up. 'No, thank you. I would be failing in *my* duty to Violet. I will stay and hear your conclusions.'

Dr Shipley shook his head. 'Is this wise? You must be careful not to over-tire yourself. Nervous exhaustion can be debilitating and highly dangerous.'

27

'I shall have regard for my health but also my responsibilities here. When we know your verdict, I must supervise Violet's removal to a more suitable room, where she can be alone.'

He frowned, obviously not welcoming the opposition. Almost sulkily he said, 'My observations will be impeded with so many around the bed, since Woodward wishes to observe also.'

'The end responsibility for everything that happens in this school is mine. I shall stay. We can both stand.' She was moving the stools as she spoke. 'Please continue.' She was disappointed in the doctor's reaction. He was belittling her in a way she did not like.

And the minister? Her head was throbbing; she no longer knew what to expect of him. If he wanted only to protect her school, why dissuade the doctor from making a bland and harmless announcement last night, straightaway? She was sure Dr Shipley would have done so, if not prevented. She should have tackled Woodward directly about his actions at the time.

Now she wanted only the truth. She said briskly, 'The minister was correct in suggesting a daylight examination. Last night, after you left, he and I noticed a wound hidden beneath the girl's hair. See.' She held the hair back yet again, her fingers steady as she lifted her face to his — and intercepted a look passing between the two men. Of what? Disquiet? Warning?

Dr Shipley was saying, 'Ah, yes.'

Hannah said, 'How could this have occurred? Might she have fallen?'

Dr Shipley hesitated. 'She could have fallen, of course and knocked her head against some protuberance as she fell. I have known it happen; a slight stumble, of little account unless the victim encounters a projecting branch or misplaced stone, and the results are unfortunately fatal. I have known this happen in the young and healthy, not merely the aged and infirm who are of course prone to falling. I believe that to be my conclusion: a fatal contusion caused by a fall.'

From being reluctant to speak at all, he was now saying too much. Perhaps intending to distract her? And had seemed almost eager to seize upon her suggestion. She wondered uneasily how far she could trust him too. Or was he merely seeking the easiest way out?

'Could the injury have been caused by a blow?' she asked.

'I suppose one might say so, but it is so unlikely as to be well-nigh impossible. A safe and secure environment, a closed community such as your admirable little school . . . '

'I would certainly hope not. But if anything like that has happened, I must know of it. I shall question everyone in the house myself as soon as I may; if Violet fell, some of the other girls may have seen it. Or any other unfortunate occurrence.' She gripped her hands together. 'And then we must inform Sir George, I believe.'

The minister spoke at last. 'Is that necessary?'

'I am right, surely, Doctor. There

must be an inquest. He is the local magistrate.'

'Miss Hannah, consider, please.' The minister was staring earnestly and directly into her eyes. Hannah found herself staring back, noting for the first time that his eyes held strange depths, and she could hardly tell whether they were blue or grey; and would you not expect brown eyes with dark hair?

She blinked, shaking her head, but he was continuing: 'We must be fully aware of the consequences of our actions. If an unlawful killing is even suspected, no doubt wrongly, how will the other girls' parents react, and understandably so? If they choose to remove their daughters, then even if we prove there was no need at all for any concern, you may have the greatest difficulty in persuading them to return. A bad reputation, however ill-deserved, tends to stick. You have such an admirable school here. In the course of my professional duties, I have rarely visited a school with such a happy and healthy atmosphere, and such an air of cheerful application. Please do not allow all this to be swept away. At least not before we have had the opportunity to discover the truth of this for ourselves.'

'Discover the truth?' Hannah said.

'Yes, Woodward,' Dr Shipley agreed. 'We are better equipped to do so than Sir George. Although a man of sense, he is always happy to be shown the way forward, rather than choosing the way himself.' He paused. 'Although he must be informed, of course.'

Hannah looked from one to the other. Could she trust either of them? Was this planned, or were they drawn together by the opportunity of the moment? Why so eager to leave Sir George out of this tragedy? Did they feel Hannah would be more likely to uncover the truth than Sir George — or less? And why should it matter to either of them?

All the same, there might be advantages in interviewing the girls herself before anyone else. Sir George had visited the school occasionally, but seemed to regard this as a duty with which he felt ill at ease, barking questions like an inspector of schools and sending the little ones into floods of terrified tears. Why did he come at all? There was no reason. And by his reactions, Hannah doubted whether he would regard her achievements here in the same glowing light that the minister and the doctor appeared to.

Regretfully, she made her decision. 'I must act correctly and be seen to be doing so. I will send Tom Turley for Sir George straightaway. I cannot justify any further delay.'

The minister was nodding. 'Even so, Sir George will hardly be rising yet. By the time he arrives, we may find evidence pointing to a conclusion that will not involve anyone else.'

Dr Shipley said, 'I agree. But for now, if you will both excuse me, I have other patients awaiting me. I will return by this afternoon, learn what you have discovered, and give my official report for the certificate of death.'

Hannah, surprised, thought the minister might protest, but Woodward merely nodded. Yes, this had to be the best decision. The doctor had not provided the strength she had hoped for. She would be better able to coax the truth from the girls than Sir George or indeed anyone else.

There was a tap at the door, and Margaret entered without waiting for her sister's response. She was red-eyed and pale but otherwise seemed composed enough, thankfully, apart from the tell-tale twitching of her fingers amongst her dark skirts. 'Are there to be lessons today? And what about Violet's class?'

'Good morning, Margaret.' The greeting was a reproof. Poor Margaret, always completely unaware of the social niceties. And now there were further decisions to be made. 'I will speak to all the girls together before lessons. And perhaps Mr Woodward will say some suitable prayers in Violet's memory? I think Lavinia can take Violet's class to begin with. Yes, Doctor, of course you must go.' She turned from agreeing that he might see himself out, to regarding her sister again. 'But before anything else, I need to talk to you, Margaret.'

3

Margaret turned from smiling wistfully after the doctor. 'To me?'

Hannah took a breath. At all costs, she must appear calm, for Margaret's sake in particular. She must fulfil Father's trust, to care for her sister. 'Yes. But not here. We need to talk about what has happened. Come with me.'

Behind her, the Reverend Woodward was clearing his throat. 'Excuse me, but if I may suggest? Would it not be advisable for another to be present? Myself — or even the doctor? I am sure we could call him back.' He added, 'In all cases, not only for your sister. I think Sir George would consider it fitting.'

Of course. What was she thinking of? Sir George might well view any private conversations with a degree of suspicion. The minister was right — but again, why was he so eager to participate? Was it purely a desire to help? And why only mention this when the doctor had left?

Margaret simpered, 'Oh, indeed. Whatever you have to say to me, Hannah, I should be more than happy to include either gentleman — or both.'

Oh, Margaret, Hannah thought in exasperated affection. Could she never understand that her eagerness was inappropriate? Last evening, which seemed so long ago now, both gentlemen had been politely attentive to her. Hannah could not consider their responses to be more than that, much as she would have wished to see Margaret settled with a suitable husband of kindness and understanding. Besides, Hannah too must accept that the time for such opportunities was past.

She nodded. 'Very well. There may be advantages in your attending.'

'Sir George, or anyone else for that matter, may wish to hear an alternative account of what has been said.'

Hannah raised her eyebrows. Did he trust her as little as she did him? Yet she had grounds for her mistrust after what she had seen, while he most certainly did not. *Be calm*, she told herself. She needed her wits about her and anger would help no one, least of all Margaret. 'I agree; that makes perfect sense. Who would dispute the word of a man of the cloth?'

He smiled, ignoring her sarcasm. 'So I have always found.'

'We will go to my study for now — although we must be brief. I cannot leave Lavinia alone with the girls for too long.'

She led the way downstairs, seating herself and Margaret before the fire, already lit by the dutiful Millie. The minister seemed disposed to stand, but she gestured to a small chair in the corner, hoping his presence would not seem too oppressive. Yet it was distracting all the same, as Margaret kept turning her head to include him in her replies.

'We have to find out what happened,' Hannah said quietly. 'And how Violet seemed to be lately. And I shall have to ask everyone the same questions. Also, this is in the nature of a preparation, as it may be that Sir George will wish to speak to you as well.'

Margaret brightened. 'Sir George? Oh, my.'

'I'm sure he will wish to speak to all of us, depending on the conclusions I draw myself, or we draw. Now, Margaret, think carefully. Do you consider that Violet had any sign of illness in the last day or so?'

Margaret paused, her head to one side, giving the simple question more consideration than was necessary. 'No, I do not think so. But there must have been, must there not? We can only assume so.'

'Did you hear of Violet suffering any accident recently?'

'I don't know what you mean.'

'A fall, maybe?'

'Oh, a fall! The very thing. I never

thought of that. A blow to the head can be most injurious, as when dear Father . . . ' Her eyes filled with tears.

'He fell because he had suffered a seizure and his heart was not strong,' Hannah said quickly. 'You know that. It was a different situation altogether.'

'I know. I'm sorry. But we were not there.' She accepted the minister's proffered handkerchief with a grateful glance and a bowed head.

'He was not alone. A good end, to be in the midst of sociable activity with friends about him. So, were you aware of Violet meeting with any such mishap? Anything at all, however slight?'

'No, but she was always hurrying, wasn't she? Not in a bouncing manner, you understand, Mr Woodward; but she had a way of slipping hither and thither. You would expect her from one direction and willy-nilly, she would appear from another. I always found it unsettling. Tripping swiftly up and down the stairs and always so quietly with it. She would give me quite a start, many a time.'

'Yes.' *And deliberately too*, Hannah suspected.

'I don't like to say she would do it purposely, knowing the state of my nerves, but sometimes I did wonder . . . '

The minister said, 'So we establish that Violet was a young woman of rapid movement — but did you witness or hear of an actual fall?'

'No. For all her speed, she was very surefooted. Like a cat, I always thought.'

'When did you last see Violet?' Woodward asked suddenly.

This was not a line of questioning Hannah had considered, and briefly she frowned at the interruption, although it made sense.

'Oh, let me see. It should have been as the girls were making ready for bed, and usually she would be supervising her girls in the east dormitory as I was helping Lavinia in the west room.'

Hannah glanced at the minister. 'Lavinia is a capable girl.' She had considered asking her to return as a pupil-teacher the following term; now that plan must be brought forward if the school was to survive at all.

'But of course,' Margaret was murmuring with another sidelong glance. 'Yesterday evening we had our little soirée. Such fun! So it will have been quite early in the evening when I last saw her. She was in the hall, and was kind enough to compliment me upon my gown. She said, 'Oh, Miss Margaret, you do look well tonight. You will be . . . '' She stopped abruptly. 'I cannot say.'

'Whisper to me,' Hannah said, hoping that the minister would not object to this. She suspected Violet's comment would be embarrassing enough as it was.

'Capturing a fine suitor!' Margaret hid the words behind her hand, her eyes wide. 'What do you think of that?'

'Er — yes. A passing remark, no more.'

'And then she said, 'You have to be

so careful with the neck and shoulders at a certain age — but that dress sets you off to perfection.' But you know, she said it with that sideways glint in her eye that Violet had at times, when you suspected she meant the exact opposite of what she had said but could never be sure. That quality of slyness that made her so provoking. You know what I mean, Hannah?'

'Indeed I do.'

'But I don't know what I might have done to provoke her spite. Oh! Do you suppose she felt she should have been dining with us? That we were keeping our fine gentlemen to ourselves?'

'That is speculation,' Hannah said hastily. 'I feel we should keep to what Violet actually said and did.'

Margaret spread her hands. 'That was all. I passed on down the stairs, feeling I had been given a fine compliment that might not be what it seemed. At the bottom, I paused and looked back. And of course she was gone from the landing so swiftly, as she

43

did. In that annoying way. You know, Violet was a most provoking girl. I should not say it, but I do not think I shall miss her overmuch.'

'No, you should not say it,' Hannah said sharply. 'And particularly not to Sir George.'

'But Hannah,' Margaret said in a reasonable tone, her pale eyes wide and innocent, 'have you not always said that truth is paramount? That without truth, the very structure of our society and all we hold dear will crumble?'

'Oh Margaret, dear, I am not asking you to lie; just to answer his questions simply and directly but without enlarging your responses with your personal opinions — which may only serve to confuse Sir George in *his* opinions.'

Margaret nodded. 'Yes, I see what you mean. Indeed I believe I do. I will not let you down. You can trust in me.' She gave a little knowing smile. 'Is my interview now at an end?'

Hannah sighed. 'This was not intended as an interview. But, yes, I believe it is.

And Margaret, as you return to the girls, please try — as I shall — to quash any gossip and speculation among them. I shall be speaking to them all together very soon.'

'And then are you to announce a day's leave from the usual lessons? In respect for Violet?'

'I will see.' She frowned. It might seem suitable, but what would the girls do instead? Free time might only lead to an undesirable atmosphere of fear and doubt.

'Of course, you do not need to tell me what you intend.' With a swish of her skirts, Margaret succeeded in expressing her displeasure at being partially excluded, and also a sense of complicity.

Hannah sighed. Her complex, irritating and lovable sister must be protected at all costs.

★   ★   ★

Hannah stood at the front of the classroom facing her pupils, all now washed, dressed and breakfasted, though pale and subdued. In happier times, this had been the library. She could picture their father sitting before the fire. But those days were gone, and she must face up to the present. She was thankful that Tom Turley had returned to say that Sir George was not yet available; he would come as soon as he was able, probably this afternoon. So she had acted correctly and yet been given a welcome respite.

'Girls, as you will all know, we had a sad happening here last night. Regrettably, Violet has died. But we must be strong and brave.'

One of the smallest, little Jenny Lee, raised her hand. 'Miss Hannah, when my little sister died, Mamma said she had gone to a better place where she could be well and happy.'

'Yes, Jenny, your mamma was quite right.' She turned to fix the minister with a firm stare. His predecessor would have made this the occasion for a lengthy sermon; and although this might well have a calming effect, she felt this was not yet the time. 'Shortly, the minister will lead us in some brief prayers for Violet. But I expect your little sister had suffered an illness before she died, Jenny? However, if Violet had been at all ill, neither I nor Miss Margaret knew of it. If any of you knew of any symptoms Violet may have had, any signs that she was feeling at all unwell, you can tell us of it. Anything at all, if she even seemed more weary than usual. Or if she had met with any mishap. A fall, perhaps?'

They all screwed up their faces intently, anxious to please. If only one of them could remember something. Hannah waited for a while, hoping.

'Never mind. If Miss Margaret and I noticed nothing, why should any of you? But if you think of anything, you will come and tell me, won't you?'

'Or Miss Margaret,' Amy Green said.

Hannah hesitated. 'It is probably best to come directly to me and not to trouble Miss Margaret. I shall be here. And there is something more. Sir

George, who always takes such an interest in the school, will be here later today and will probably wish to speak to you, as I have. Or one or two of you at a time. But I shall be in attendance. Just speak clearly and tell what you remember, as best you are able. There is nothing to worry about.' She hoped that was true. It would be. She would make it true. She smiled her reassurance. 'Now, please continue with the lessons, Lavinia, as planned, and do not worry if concentration is lacking today or if any of the girls seem to prefer a time of quiet reflection.'

Her measured and practical approach seemed to be having the effect hoped for. She nodded, leaving the room to Lavinia; only on reaching the corridor did she allow her shoulders to slump as she sought the sanctuary of the study.

'Well done,' the minister said.

She had forgotten him but he was still here. Her shoulders shot back into place. 'It was necessary. I cannot be seen to be weak, however I may be feeling.' She was glaring at him — another unwelcome reaction on her part when she must aim for constant calm, as so many people were depending on her to give an example of strength. 'I was not expecting criticism.'

'I was not offering any.'

'Or praise.' She half-smiled grimly at herself. 'I am sorry. Of course you are not offering either. I think I am anticipating what may well be Sir George's response. But always my first priority has to be to my pupils.' *And Margaret, of course.*

'I should not worry about Sir George unduly. I can vouch for you.'

Hannah raised her brows. 'And he will accept your word where he will not take mine? As a woman, I presume.'

'No, that's not what I meant. If my opinion would carry more weight in my position as minister, then we should make use of that.'

'I'm sure Sir George will accept my view. He has been a friend of my family for years; he knew my father well. He knows me to be of upright character. I can depend upon his accepting my word.' She wished she felt as certain as she sounded. She had depended on him before, five years ago. She shook her head. No point in dwelling upon what might have been. If she had married Sir George, she told herself stoutly, she would never have enjoyed the independence and sense of achievement gained by opening the school.

The minister was saying, 'I'm sure you are right. You are better acquainted with Sir George, and how he might think, than a newcomer to the neighbourhood.'

The study door began to open in a series of small jerking movements that Hannah recognised. 'One moment, Margaret,' she called, 'I shall be with you shortly.'

The door was flung open. 'I am sure I would not wish to interrupt anything of importance,' Margaret cried.

Hannah stared at her. As so often happened, she had underestimated her sister's reactions to these unusual circumstances. Margaret had seemed to be acting with sense and propriety. She found herself glancing at the minister to see how he might be taking this outburst.

He said carefully, 'No, I must be going, of course. I am occupying too much of Miss Hannah's time as it is, and I do have an hour of chapel business this afternoon. But if I may, I will return when Sir George arrives, to support you in any way I can. I am sure I will see his horse — but if not, send someone over for me and I shall come at once. Please.'

Margaret's face was tight and pink. Hannah placed a restraining hand on her arm as the minister took his leave, although he was hardly through the front door before Margaret could restrain herself no longer.

'Sometimes I cannot understand you, Hannah. I was so happy about the prospect of our little dinner party and what might come of it. Even better that

Sir George and Lady Foxcroft could not attend, for we have no hopes there now, and Lady Foxcroft does so seek the gentlemen's attention with her sighs and simpers. Though inviting her might well ensure a return invitation when they first make use of their newly built ballroom. I hope so.'

Hannah did not try to stop her. The door was tightly shut and it was better, she knew, to allow Margaret to pour everything out. When she ceased, the storm might be quelled, replaced by her more customary disposition.

Margaret turned on the rug, wringing her hands. 'And it began well, it truly did; but then — oh, Hannah, I know you have to seek a husband too, but it is not fair of you to make a point of shining so, that the guests hang upon your every word. You know I am not clever, and I need to have little opportunities made for my small offerings; and in the past you have often remembered that. But last night there was nothing for me. Nothing.'

Hannah opened her mouth in surprise. In spite of Violet's ill-advised remark, Hannah had not suspected that Margaret's hopes were still set fruitlessly upon marriage. She had assumed that like her, Margaret had given up all such thoughts long ago, with Sir George's defection. She murmured half to herself, 'We are both too old now, Margaret to have any such valid hopes.'

'Nonsense. If you truly believe that, why set up your little party? I was so pleased. Previously, whenever I have asked for a little social diversion, you have made the excuse that the school was taking all our resources and energy. You kept putting me off — and at last you were keeping your promise to me and to Father, as I thought. And if it weren't enough that you took all the gentlemen's attention last night for yourself, when Violet was discovered you packed me off to bed with the children so *you* could have the company of the doctor and the minister. Why could I not share the vigil? And this

53

morning it still goes on. You did not want me to come in just now. You cannot deny that. You were closeted with the minister, and when I entered all the same, he set off home immediately seeing that his cosy little tête-à-tête was spoilt.'

'That is enough, Margaret,' Hannah said in an icy tone she did not know she possessed.

Margaret stopped, open-mouthed, her face as white as if Hannah had slapped her. Hannah winced as if she indeed had. But her surge of anger had swept her usual patience away. 'Margaret, you must understand we are in trouble financially. I cannot believe you do not appreciate the gravity of our position. Manipulating events to be alone with the gentlemen was the last thing on my mind, believe me. I am amazed and horrified you should think that of me.'

Margaret's voice was sulky. 'I know what I see. I see life as it is.'

'No, Margaret, you do not. The

dinner party was entirely to seek recommendations for further pupils.'

Margaret ignored this. 'I see more than you. And as for Violet, perhaps she deserved what happened to her.'

Hannah stared at her. 'What do you mean?' She had her own suspicions about last night, but she must be careful not to breathe a word of them to Margaret. Not before Sir George arrived and drew his own conclusions — otherwise, who knew what muddle Margaret might come out with.

'Sudden fevers? Accidental falls? You must think I'm stupid. I see. I listen. Poor, stupid Margaret who cannot be taken into her sister's confidence. But I know, all the same. Do not worry, Hannah — I will not betray you, despite your lack of trust in me. I know how to keep faith. Even though Violet was no better than she should be, and little better than a slut. Sir George will not hear a word of it from me.' Margaret flounced over to the door.

'Margaret! What are you talking about?'

'Well, that's for you to discover, is it not, with your clever questions? Work it out with the help of your fellow investigator. But perhaps he knows more than he is telling you. Have you thought of that?' Margaret slammed the door behind her with a hysterical laugh.

Hannah's hands were trembling. She should be used to poor Margaret's outbursts by now, but she had never experienced such a vitriolic attack. As if the sentiments had been building up within Margaret's head for some time. Weeks. Months, even?

Hannah knew she was losing her grasp upon events. Even as she strove to attain some kind of order, the truth slipped away further.

4

This time yesterday, apart from her financial situation, there had been nothing more for Hannah to worry about than whether the beef would be medium rare — and now everything had changed. Rightly or wrongly, she was being swept from one decision to the next.

Talking to Margaret was one thing, although whether she had handled the interview to achieve the best outcome was doubtful — but could she justify talking to anyone else? Yes, she must. She must not waste this gift of the extra time she had been granted until Sir George arrived. It was more than fortunate he was not yet here.

There were also the servants to consider. And what about the minister? Yes, indeed, what about him? He might be easy to talk to and good at listening, but that was all part of his calling; she had liked him from the first when he had replaced the aging Reverend Howard. He visited the school far more often than his predecessor, and with an endearing enthusiasm. Before last night, Hannah had welcomed him as an ally. Even so, liking him, she must be even more wary.

Leave that for now. She set off to the kitchen where by now Joan Copley the cook, and Millie Garforth should be preparing the usual simple luncheon. In the hall, however, she found Millie approaching the stairs with a tray. *Oh no.* In her exasperation, her voice became sharper than she intended. 'Millie, you have more than enough to do without taking food up to Miss Hoyle. If she is well enough to eat, she is surely well enough to come down.'

Millie nodded. 'I don't mind it, Miss Hannah, for the poor thing. The way she was treated was shameful. And Lady Foxcroft has sent her some comfits over again. Guilt, Mrs Copley says when they dismissed her after all those faithful years caring for Sir George; she said I might as well take her something to eat at the same time, to tempt her appetite.' Millie stopped abruptly. 'Oh, and the man from the hall brought a note for you as well, on the table there. I would have brought it in but didn't want to disturb you.'

Hannah nodded. 'Quite right, Millie. Thank you.' She frowned. 'A note for me? From Sir George?'

'No, from Lady Foxcroft; and her man is waiting for a reply. He's in the kitchen.' She ran lightly up the stairs and Hannah could hear her feet pattering up the flight to the attic rooms. To begin with, Miss Hoyle had slept in a dormitory as part of her duties, but had been forced to retire so often with her headaches that a room of her own had become necessary.

'You are too soft-hearted,' Margaret had said. 'Why shouldn't she work like we do, since she's here?' Yes, indeed. Once, she had hoped Miss Hoyle might assist in the teaching of French and Drawing to be added to the prospectus as remunerative extras per quarter.

Hannah tore the sheet open. Of course, this was merely a profuse apology for being prevented by the inclement weather from attending the evening before. She skimmed the fulsome and doubtless insincere phrases. Why should this need a reply? She was almost folding it again when the final sentences caught her eye. *Be assured of my constant support as I do so admire your brave venture with your school. Even if failure is imminent, please come to me for help.*

Whatever could Lady Foxcroft mean by that? Before last night, Hannah had never even hinted of failure. Not to anyone. Wishful thinking maybe. She smiled grimly. Well, the servant must return empty-handed for now. Hannah did not want him hanging around here, listening out for useful information to carry back, with or without a letter.

Too late, no doubt. Lady Foxcroft's man was standing by the rear door, his face alive with interest.

The cook turned to her, her usually cheerful and rounded face now suitably glum. 'We thought it best to carry on as usual, since no one had told us any different. The breakfast was needed just the same, wasn't it?'

'Of course. Thank you.' She turned to the manservant from the hall. 'There is no reply at present. I will send one over later.'

He paused as if about to object, but touched his forehead and went out.

Hannah gave a relieved sigh. 'That was exactly right, Joan, and what I would have expected of you. But I wish to interrupt for a few moments. This sad occurrence has taken us all by surprise — but I wondered whether you might know if Violet had been feeling like her usual herself over the past few days? Was she eating as usual, for instance? I thought you might have noticed.'

'But of course I did, Miss Hannah, none better. Violet was as thin as a lath and ate like a pony. She was always slipping in here for an extra bit of bread and cheese or anything that was going. And not always asking either, thinking I wouldn't notice. But we always knew, didn't we, Millie? Miss Violet thought herself very clever. As if I would forget how I'd left a spoon in a pan.'

'Her appetite wasn't too good before the Christmas holiday,' Millie put in suddenly. 'We both said so. You said she might be sickening for something. In fact, you said — '

'Never mind what I said; that's no kind of fact at all. What I said and you said down here passes only for idle gossip. That's not what Miss Hannah is wanting to hear.'

'No, please — it may well be useful,' Hannah protested. 'Millie?'

But Millie was shaking her head. Hannah decided she would not press the matter for now. She left the subject and explained about Sir George.

'Oh! You think he'll want to talk to us?'

'He may not. Only if he should, I did not wish you to be worried or upset. It will merely be a matter of routine. It may even suffice that I have spoken with you myself.'

Joan sniffed. 'There's no knowing, is there, with anything to do with the law. But don't worry, Miss Hannah, I'm not easily upset. And we won't let you down. We shall be circumspect.' She nodded in a meaningful manner.

'Oh, no. I wish you to tell the truth.'

'And we understand that. Both of us. Don't we, Millie?'

'Yes,' Millie whispered, looking from one to the other.

'Well, thank you.' As Hannah left the room, she wondered whether her little chat had wrought more harm than help. At least she could take pride in the women's loyalty.

She was passing through the hall when the bell jangled harshly, making her jump, and Millie came running with a look of terror. They arrived at the door together. Surely it could not be Sir

George already — and ringing the bell in such a way?

But it was, and he was striding forwards to brush past her before she had a chance to stand back and welcome him in. There was no sign of his customary expression of good-humoured laziness.

'What is going on here? Why was I not sent for earlier?'

Hannah stared at him. 'You were not at home. I sent a message. You were not available.' And did he not know of his wife's letter?

'Your message gave no indication of urgency. My servants know to alert me at once in such circumstances. They would have sent after me and I would have returned immediately. I have been all the way to answer a summons from Sir Joseph Steading only to find he did not send for me at all.' He glared at Hannah as if the fault was hers.

She frowned. 'I'm sorry; I don't know why any of this happened.' She tried to recall what she had told Tom to say. 'I suppose I did not want to cause panic. But Tom Turley knew his errand was important.' She said slowly, half to herself, 'I have not yet spoken to Tom in the course of my enquiries. Perhaps you might care to ask him? I have not yet discovered anything of note from the other servants or Violet's fellow pupils.'

'What is this? What are you talking about?'

'I am afraid that Violet, my senior pupil-teacher, is dead. Surely you knew that?'

'Yes, I know it now. But only because I received a message from Dr Shipley on returning from my wasted journey.'

'Ah, the doctor. Of course.' Hannah tried to smile. 'We cannot discuss this in the hall. I may have been remiss; but we have had a most distressing time of it, you understand. Please come into my study.'

Naturally, Dr Shipley should have been the one to inform Sir George, but surely he had agreed to wait until the afternoon? And at first he had seemed reluctant to admit any irregularity in Violet's death; Hannah had been the one to alert him to that sinister wound. Perhaps the doctor was regretting his initial reaction and was now trying to make amends.

'It was perfectly proper for Dr Shipley to notify you,' she said quietly. 'And if my servant has been at fault, I shall speak to him. But to me, it is more important that a valued member of my school is now dead. My concern is for her, and to discover the truth.'

Sir George glared at her. She could not tell what he was thinking. She could hardly make sense of her own thoughts.

He said, 'Naturally, we all wish to know the truth.' His piercing stare did not falter.

Hannah felt her cheek muscles twitching and strove to control them. Surely he did not suspect her of trying to conceal something? 'You must view the body immediately,' she said briskly. 'Then you may draw your own conclusions.' She winced inwardly at having to refer to poor Violet in this way, but she could not give way to weakness.

She rose and led the way upstairs. At the dormitory door, Sir George placed a restraining hand on her arm. 'I can do this alone. You have been through enough.'

She shook her head. 'This night has been something I would never wish to repeat, but the worst must be past now. And there are aspects where I particularly need your opinion.'

Indeed, Violet now seemed almost peaceful. The laying-out had been done with sensitivity by the experienced Peggy Kershaw from the village, and Violet lay pale and calm with her hands arranged on her chest. No sign now of that sly smile, making you think the worst of her.

Hannah sighed. She had been convinced Violet was good at heart. Given time, she was sure she could have succeeded with her. Giving the girl responsibility to show her faith and trust in her had been the start of it. All wasted.

'Yes,' Sir George said, his voice gruff. 'I see. Perhaps I should have viewed her before the laying-out but, no help for that now.'

There was no point in arguing about that again. 'The minister had notified Mrs Kershaw and told her to come. I saw no purpose in sending her away. And Dr Shipley, the minister and I all saw her as she was first discovered. Indeed, at first the doctor was inclined to attribute the death to natural causes, but as he may have told you he will return and give us his certificate of death now you have seen her. You see, there is a wound on her forehead.' She straightened her spine, stepped forward and again lifted the limp hair. 'Here. As if she had fallen, maybe. I hesitate to suggest a blow, though I suppose it might be possible.'

'Surely not in a well-run establishment such as yours?' Sir George twisted his fingers in his neck cloth.

'I would have hoped not.' She closed her eyes, seeking inner strength. 'But it seems a rough wound unlikely to be gained inside, and Violet's shoes were wet. See, they are still damp. And also there are faint marks on her throat, which may be bruising. Another person may have been involved.'

Sir George stared down, leaning forward. 'That is most unfortunate. I may have to speak to the coroner.'

Hannah took a deep breath. 'This is why we need your advice and presence. Obviously we do not know how to proceed.'

'It is not for you to know.' Sir George's tone was sharp. 'But I am here now and will attend to everything.'

'Not quite everything,' Hannah said. 'We have sent to Violet's father, of course. And I began the process of asking the children if Violet did indeed fall yesterday. But maybe I should have asked them if she had been involved in a squabble or something similar.'

Sir George looked horrified. 'This is

remiss in you, Hannah. Perhaps this establishment is not so well run after all. And you have obviously questioned the children prematurely.'

'Children can forget so easily. I wished to talk to them while yesterday was still fresh in their minds.'

'Also it was hardly suitable to question them alone. I will only have your word for what was said.'

'Oh, but I was not. I am sorry, I omitted to say that the minister was with me.' She stopped abruptly, wondering how reliable the minister's testimony might be since his actions had been suspicious to say the least.

Sir George, however, had no such doubts. His face lightened. 'Ah, the minister. Good. That puts a different light on the matter. He will be able to verify your findings.'

'He too will be returning shortly.'

'Good. I shall begin talking to the children myself while we wait. Individually, of course.'

'If I may suggest, not individually. As

you will have noticed on previous occasions, the children are very much in awe of you.'

Sir George frowned. 'Even so.' As if he thought she was trying to conceal something.

'Well, I must be present.'

'I do not consider that necessary. You may even hinder my search for the truth of what has happened.'

Hannah said firmly, 'I have a responsibility to all the girls. Their parents and guardians have placed their trust in me, to care for them.'

'A trust that seems to have been sadly misplaced.'

'No one is more aware of that than I am. Or regrets it as much. So I must take steps to put things right.'

They glared at each other. To her surprise, Sir George turned away first, muttering, 'Oh, very well.'

'My study will be suitable, I believe?'

He followed her again without further comment. As he seated himself in the chair Hannah usually used, however, he said, 'Naturally I must begin with you.'

'With me? Yes, of course you must.' Foolishly, she had not expected it. She blundered into her account without waiting for his questions. 'I heard screams. I hurried at once to the far dormitory, led by the sound.'

'Were you asleep?'

'No. I was . . . thinking about the school and its future.'

'At what time did this happen?'

'Oh. I didn't look at the clock. But I had retired at around midnight I believe, having made certain that our guests were suitably provided for. The snow had stopped, but the ground was treacherous and there was thick fog. They both opted to accept our offer of accommodation for the night.' She recalled Margaret's obvious delight, while Hannah herself had only been concerned that the rooms might not be suitable.

Sir George nodded. 'Regrettably, it seems Lady Foxcroft was correct in declining your invitation, although at the last minute.'

'Yes, so it would seem.' Hannah began to relax a little. Naturally, Sir George must take his legal duties seriously. Now he was seemingly more sympathetic, and remained so while she explained what had happened and what she had seen.

'Thank you. One more matter: if you were still awake when you heard the screams, did you hear anything else previously?'

'What do you mean?'

Sir George shrugged. 'Footsteps, doors opening and closing.'

'You mean, anyone who could have attacked Violet?' Hannah considered his question. 'No, I didn't. Everything was quiet.' She bit her lip. Was now the time to tell him about what she had seen from the windows, and the concealed footprints?

'Good,' Sir George said again. 'That will suffice. I will begin with the oldest girl — Lavinia, I believe?'

'I think it would be better to begin with the younger ones. Seeing the others leaving the classroom at intervals can only lead to speculation and distress for them. By the time their turn comes, they will be highly nervous and upset, when I have succeeded in calming them.'

'Oh, very well. But only after I have spoken to Lavinia. She must be first.'

'I will fetch her.'

'No; please send your maidservant for her. I do not wish you to speak with her again before I do.'

Hannah raised her eyebrows but rang the bell as he had asked. When Millie appeared, however, Sir George interrupted before Hannah had a chance to speak. 'Since you are here, I should like you to tell me whether you saw or heard anything untoward last night.'

Millie looked at Hannah and shook her head.

'Good. As I thought.' He nodded to Hannah. 'Let us continue.'

Was that all? Hannah frowned slightly

as she told Millie to fetch Lavinia. And yet considering the exchange she had witnessed in the kitchen, maybe it was just as well. At eighteen, poor Millie was little older than Lavinia, and just as likely to be fearful.

'Come in,' she called as Lavinia tapped at the door. 'You remember I told you Sir George might wish to speak with all of you?'

'Better that I handle this,' Sir George said.

'Certainly.' She managed to give no sign his interruption had unsettled her. Did he think she would try to guide Lavinia's account in some way? She had known him all her life, but was beginning to wonder whether she knew him as well as she thought. His responses seemed so erratic, veering from the cautious to the over-simplified. No wonder Lavinia also seemed fearful, glancing up at Sir George and then away again. Or was at least giving an appearance of fear. Hannah looked at her sharply.

Sir George cleared his throat and spoke softly. 'Miss Lavinia, do not be afraid. You are not in any kind of trouble. We merely wish to discover what happened last night, as far as we may.'

Lavinia's pretty face was impassive, dark eyes wide and expressionless. 'Yes, sir.'

'Pray sit on this stool here. This is in the nature of a friendly exchange, that is all.'

It was difficult to tell whether this attempt to place Lavinia at her ease had succeeded or not. With Lavinia, it was always so.

'Well then, my dear — tell me what occurred yesterday evening, as far as you recall.'

Lavinia's voice was low and soft. 'Beginning at what time?'

'From when you think anything significant occurred. No, no — that does not help you. Did you speak to Violet that evening?'

'I am sure I must have done. We are

such a small school. I spoke to her frequently. And everyone else.'

'And what did you say?'

'I think we were discussing the supper party and the inclement weather. And whether the guests who had arrived would be able to leave.'

This all sounded harmless enough, but Hannah was experiencing a faint unease, although she could not have said why.

'And of course,' Lavinia continued, 'we were responsible, in the absence of Miss Hannah and Miss Margaret, for seeing all the girls to their beds quietly. We knew there must be no disturbance to annoy the supper.' There was a slight inflection, almost mocking.

Had Sir George picked up on that? Hannah wondered if her own feelings were falsely alert and she was finding hidden meanings where none existed. *Bad enough,* she thought, *that I found it difficult to hold an impartial opinion of Violet; now I find myself admitting a similar dislike of Lavinia — and when I must be fair to all of them. Their futures are in my hands; and if any of the girls do not turn out to be a credit to the school, the failing will be mine, not theirs. And now Violet has no future and her character is fixed for all eternity.* She added sadly, *I could have done more.*

Lavinia was continuing with her recital as if she had learned it by rote. 'Everything was in order in my room when I blew out the candle, and I could hear no further sound from the other. We made a little game of it, Violet and I, with the younger ones, to see which room could be quiet first. To gain praise when Miss Hannah made her nightly round. Or Miss Margaret, of course.'

'And Miss Hannah made her round as usual?'

Lavinia made a sidelong glance. 'As often as not, none of us would hear her. Sometimes I was aware of her entrance, shielding the candle with her hand. And she always whispers, 'Goodnight, girls,' whether anyone is awake to hear or not.'

'Did you hear her last night?'

'No.' Lavinia sounded quite definite. 'I told the girls she would come to quieten them, but I didn't expect her, knowing she would have other concerns.'

Hannah frowned. Even so, she had intended going. She remembered mounting the stairs in her little worn satin, the flimsy shawl around her shoulders hardly providing a barrier against the cold. Usually she would be in the practical dark green, high-necked serge of everyday. She said, 'No. I had to go to the kitchen. I intended going later, but I did not.'

Sir George smiled. 'And you would have been serving a good wine, I trust? One of your father's best?'

'Yes. A claret.'

Sir George sighed. 'That was my most profound regret in refusing your invitation. Your father knew his wine.' He shook his head, smiling; and politely, she smiled with him. 'No one

79

better than I to know the strength and efficacy of your father's clarets.' His tone darkened abruptly. 'It is possible, is it not, that the wine might have blunted your awareness, Miss Hannah?'

Hannah's smile froze. This was hardly an appropriate question, particularly in Lavinia's presence. 'I can assure you I did not take enough to blunt my faculties. I have always been abstemious with wine, and there was water available, in the French manner favoured by my mother. No, I am taking my time in replying, Sir George, to ensure that I answer you correctly. I know how important it is that we all do so.' The stray thought entered her mind that she was glad he had not married her. Today he seemed irritable and unpredictable in a way she could not like. She felt an easing, at last, of the bitterness she had concealed for so long.

'No matter.' Sir George shifted in his chair. He jerked his head abruptly in Lavinia's direction as if trying to catch her out. 'So who was it, Lavinia, who discovered the unfortunate deceased?'

Lavinia did not flinch. 'I did.'

'Thus it was your screams that roused the house.'

'Yes.'

Hannah looked at Lavinia as she sat quietly with her hands folded in her lap. It was difficult to imagine that anyone so collected would respond with a scream. If this had occurred to Sir George however, he did not remark on it.

He said instead, 'How could this be? You have already told me you were in charge of the girls in the *other* room. How did *you* discover this tragedy?' He sat back with a small smile of triumph, his trap neatly sprung.

'I thought I heard a noise in the corridor. I went out to investigate. We had been warned particularly against causing any disturbance, and I thought one of the little ones might be running about. Sleep-walking perhaps. I could see clearly with the light of the moonlight on the snow that all *my* girls were in their beds.'

'You were not asleep?'

'I had tried to stay awake. I have been newly given this position of trust. I am eager to prove my worth. If not one of my girls, I thought it must be one of Violet's. I needed to quieten whoever it was.'

Hannah thought, *And to try to catch Violet out?*

'When you opened the door,' asked Sir George, 'what did you see?'

She hesitated slightly, almost as if wondering what he might wish her to say. 'Nothing.'

'Or hear?'

'I thought I could hear steps down in the hall, too heavy to be one of the children and so no concern of mine. So I went to the other room to make sure everything there was all right; that the sounds had not disturbed any of the children, and to ensure Violet was at her post and all her girls safe.'

Hannah opened her mouth to interrupt and thought better of it as Sir George nodded. Why should Violet not be at her post? But Lavinia was continuing, as if in answer to Hannah's frown. 'I was tired; I did not intend sleeping but may have woken suddenly. I expect my actions were not as logical as one might wish in that situation.' A swift glance of the dark eyes from beneath her lids. 'Is that not so?' So swift that the significance of her glance could easily be missed or misinterpreted; but Hannah drew breath sharply and Sir George gave a small nod and a smile as if knowing the glance was directed at him.

Hannah clenched her hands, keeping her face impassive and knowing she had made serious errors of judgement in not keeping a tight enough rein upon her little community. She had never realised it might be necessary. Thank goodness she had seen this aspect of Lavinia's character before any harm was done. A thought chilled her. *Or more harm.*

She could be quiet no longer. 'And then?'

'I saw Violet asleep, as I thought, and

went to speak to her. I wanted to know if she had heard anything. I thought she was merely pretending to be asleep.'

'Why did you think that?' Sir George asked.

Hannah did not want to hear the answer but knew she must. And there was no stopping the beautiful, even tones. 'Because I thought *she* might know all too well who had been hurrying through the corridors at night.' A studied pause, for maximum effect, both hands clasped to her face, eyes wide with horror. '*I* do not know who it was. But I believe I had heard the steps of a murderer.'

5

Hannah swayed a little in her chair, but it was Lavinia who was receiving Sir George's attention. He was ringing the bell, calling for 'A glass of water, and quickly now.' Fighting dizziness, Hannah took her vinaigrette from her pocket and wafted it beneath Lavinia's nose and then her own. Millie came with the water and Sir George again took charge; the maidservant must help Lavinia back upstairs to lie down.

'No,' Lavinia said weakly. 'I am fully recovered now. I can return to my duties.'

'Indeed you will not,' Hannah said. What havoc would she cause if she continued with this performance within the classroom? Because she was certain they had witnessed a performance — and one that might almost be admired. If there should be any shreds of truth within her account, however, the accompanying dramatics had obscured them. She said, 'You may go and sit with Violet for me, please. She was your friend; I should have offered you this opportunity earlier. She is in the small room at the end of the landing kept for the sick.'

Sir George seemed impressed by Lavinia's account, however. As she left them, he said, 'It seems we have our culprit. A male intruder.'

'But how could this intruder gain entrance?' Hannah demanded. 'The minister checked all the doors and windows; it was almost his first thought.'

'And found nothing? Yes, I shall ask him myself. But there are many ways in which entrance might have been gained. By the key, by a door left unlocked by arrangement . . .'

'Sir George! Please do not make such allegations without substantial evidence.' Was she protecting Violet's reputation fruitlessly when it seemed likely there was none to protect? But Violet's reputation was bound inextricably with that of the school itself. Her fall from grace would bring the school tumbling with her. *And deservedly so,* Hannah thought bitterly, *because I should have known about it — or at least suspected.*

'We have made advances,' Sir George said. 'This is most satisfactory.' He seemed more composed now, continuing, 'I had better see the other girls in Violet's charge; although if Miss Lavinia is correct, they were slumbering throughout the dreadful events and will tell us nothing. But we shall see.'

Hannah rose. 'I will fetch them,' she said firmly.

Perhaps Sir George was still musing upon Lavinia's revelations, because he merely waved a hand in acknowledgment.

Hannah paused in the hall, welcoming the opportunity for a few moments to herself. Events were moving too quickly. However she tried to regain control, everything slid out of her grasp in a dozen spirals of smoke.

She sighed and then started as the doorbell jangled almost over her head. 'It is all right, Millie,' she called, 'I am here,' though doubting herself even as she reached for the door handle. Should she be cautious, on this day of strange events? But no. 'Mr Woodward!' Her face broke into a spontaneous smile; she found she was greeting the minister as an ally, trusted or not.

The minister's answering smile seemed wary. 'I have only just received your message that Sir George is here. I am sorry; I have been . . . well, circumstances forced me to be elsewhere.'

'There is no need to explain. Obviously clergymen have many demands on their time.' She hurried on, 'Sir George has been here for a while, and I welcome your presence. You were right — he is most unwilling to ask my opinion, still less pay attention to anything I say. In fact, he is unhappy that we spoke to anyone before he arrived. He seemed reassured when I told him you had been present — but not completely.'

Mr Woodward nodded gravely. Was she imagining a reluctance to meet her eyes? As he strode along the corridor with his head bowed, there seemed little sign of their earlier camaraderie in adversity, which she had found so helpful and reassuring.

She opened the door of the small parlour. 'The Reverend Woodward, Sir George.'

'Ah, good.' Sir George's face lightened as they shook hands. 'A most regrettable matter. Most distressing. Shall we ring for refreshment?'

'Thank you, no,' answered the minister.

'Are you able to join me in this difficult task? I own I would value your contribution. As an unbiased observer, you know.'

Hannah said yet again, 'Excuse me, but to join *us*. I must be present as a chaperone; the girls' parents would rightly demand nothing less.'

Sir George shrugged her interruption away. 'Oh, very well. I was — we were — just about to speak to those children who shared Violet's dormitory, Woodward. We have already spoken to Miss Lavinia, who raised the alarm. A most interesting account; pity you were not here for it.'

'And you have also interviewed me,' Hannah said. 'Naturally you will be speaking to the minister too. Will you not?' She was becoming impatient with the way Sir George was proceeding, although as the local representative of the law it was his right.

'What's that? I beg your pardon?' Sir George seemed displeased.

'Because at the time, I was present in the building myself,' the minister said quickly.

Hannah nodded. Yes, indeed. A man's steps, if Lavinia was to be believed. No sign of an entry by force. And he and the doctor had already been present within the building. Would the minister admit to seeing the sets of footprints — and to what he did next?

Woodward said, 'But I am afraid I cannot add anything of any great moment — or not from what I witnessed myself. Dr Shipley and I were sharing adjacent rooms near the end of the corridor. I heard the screams and came out, but Miss Hannah was in the corridor before me, and before the doctor opened his door.'

'The screams must have been very loud,' Sir George said.

'They were. The first, single scream was quickly joined by others and loud sobbing from the little ones.'

'I may need to ratify this. For my own satisfaction, you understand. I am not doubting your word, sir. Your rooms were on the upper corridor?'

'Yes.'

'So there would have been no need for either yourself or the doctor to make use of the stairs?'

'That is correct.'

Hannah nodded, although surely Sir George had not believed Lavinia?

Perhaps he considered these two professional men must be above reproach and wished to make that clear.

'And you heard nothing else before the first scream?'

'No; I was asleep.' Woodward paused, looking from Hannah to Sir George. 'What exactly do you think I might have heard?'

Sir George pursed his mouth. 'It pains me to tell you, but Miss Lavinia has stated she heard footsteps on the stairs and in the corridor. A man's heavy tread.'

'No. I was heavily asleep. I woke with a start, I recall.'

'Ah. Indeed.' Sir George was staring into the fire. 'You have only recently arrived to live here, but I presume you must have met Miss Violet, the victim?'

'Yes, on more than one occasion.'

'What opinion did you form of the young woman?'

'Opinion?' Mr Woodward seemed at

a loss for words. Hannah noticed the tension in the back of his neck. Did he suspect a trap? Both men seemed to have momentarily forgotten her.

'Yes. You must surely have had one. Or was she such a nonentity that you did not?'

'No, no. Certainly not that. I found her . . . ' His eyes passed over Hannah's face without seeing her. 'Always polite and dutiful. I visited the school frequently, as a local minister and because Mr Brockley and his family had attended my chapel. In general I saw her as one member of the school, not as an individual.'

'But she was a pupil-teacher, I gather. And you obviously knew who she was.'

Woodward coughed. 'I know all the girls by name. How else am I to be responsible for their spiritual welfare?'

Sir George leaned forward. 'And did you sense anything further in her? An inappropriate regard maybe? For doubtless a manse and a fine stipend will always prove popular with young ladies.'

Woodward gave an incredulous laugh. 'No, certainly not. She was very young.'

'Seventeen, I believe,' Sir George said.

Hannah said, 'I cannot see where this is leading us. Fascinating as the minister's views on character might be, I suggest we proceed with interviewing the children. Otherwise, lunchtime will be upon us. May I begin with two of the younger ones? Amy and Lucy Green, who are sisters.'

'Hmm? Oh yes, pray do so. I am to ask whether the girls in the dormitory heard anything of note last night, Woodward. That is my main query. Miss Hannah seems determined they did not.'

Hannah moved a chair slightly. 'If I may suggest, I shall sit here with the children beside me so I may reassure them.'

'I expect so. As long as you do not try

and lead them in any way.'

'No, Sir George, I shall not do that.' Pompous, overbearing man. She had had a fortunate escape.

As Hannah entered the classroom, she smiled gently at the faces that swivelled fearfully to meet hers. Today they would startle at the slightest thing, there was no doubt of that. She spoke almost cheerfully. 'Amy and Lucy, come with me, my dears, for a moment or two. You are good, clever children who have been very brave today.'

Lucy clung to her skirts as they walked along the corridor. Hannah could almost feel the child's terror. But if she told them not to worry, her words would have the opposite effect.

'It is only Sir George,' she said lightly. 'You have met him a dozen times. He is not used to children, so we must help him whenever we can. He fails miserably when he tries to speak to them. Do you think you can do that for me?'

Intrigued by the idea of a failing in a

grown man, they nodded. As they entered the study together, it was fortunate that Sir George did not know how she had achieved the air of cautious enquiry now evident in Amy, while even Lucy was not staring down at her feet.

'Aha!' Sir George said. 'Hello. You are to stand by Miss Hannah here. I wish to speak to you.' Hardly giving Hannah enough time to be seated and draw the girls towards her, he began straightaway. 'Last night, my dears, what did you see and hear? Speak up. Do not be frightened. We are not ogres who might devour you.'

Ogres? Amy looked round fearfully. Lucy gave a stifled sob. Hannah said gently, 'Last night, do you remember going to bed in the usual way? Can you tell us what happened?'

The girls clung to her hands, glancing briefly at the fearsome gentleman who was now frowning with impatience. Would they pluck up the courage to speak at all?

She said gently, 'Was the routine the same as usual?'

'Yes,' Amy whispered at last.

'And was Violet there?'

'Yes.'

'All the time?'

They both looked up at her. Another glance to Sir George. 'Yes.'

'This is useless,' Sir George muttered. 'We may as well send them back. They are too young.'

'No, wait,' Hannah said. 'Did anything different happen during the night?'

They both shook their heads, their chins swivelling from side to side.

'Nothing at all?'

The heads continued to shake.

'So you went to bed. And slept.'

The heads wobbled and stopped. 'Yes.'

'And did you hear anything?'

Amy stood on her toes to whisper in Hannah's ear.

'What? What was that?' Sir George barked.

'Only the screaming, Sir George,' Hannah said.

'Come now, Miss Hannah; this will not do. They must not speak through you. Tell them to speak up.'

'Screaming,' Amy muttered.

Sir George leaned forward. 'And did no one come into the room when you were all in bed? Did you not hear anyone? A man's voice? A man's steps? The door opening or closing?'

The two heads were shaking as if they would wobble off and away. Sir George sat back in his chair, hands flat on his knees with an air of defeat.

'Yes, yes. There is nothing to be gained by further questions here.'

Hannah took their hands. 'I shall bring someone else. Is that not your wish?' she added, as Sir George was frowning again.

'Not yet. Put them in the corridor and let them run to their class. I wish to speak to you again.'

'Indeed I will not. The girls are upset. I shall make sure I entrust them to my sister's care.' She did not wait for Sir George's dismissive gesture but took the girls from the room, glad yet again of a few moments on her own. Back in the classroom, however, Margaret did not help matters by demanding sharply who was required next; so the whole class needed to be quietened and reassured yet again.

As Hannah re-entered the small parlour, she interrupted a muttered exchange taking place between the two men. They stopped abruptly. Sir George said, 'Ah, there you are.' His sudden heartiness was not convincing. 'So what did you make of our voluble little witnesses?'

'As I expected from the few words I had with them earlier, they would seem to have nothing to contribute to your enquiry. This has been an ordeal for them and I am glad it is over.' Hannah hoped it was. Knowing the girls as she did, she had a faint feeling of unease about their responses. Towards the end, they had become strangely vehement.

'Yes, yes — but are they telling the truth?'

'The truth? Yes, of course. I doubt whether those two little girls would be capable of lying.'

'And no one could have threatened them in any way? Or frightened them into responding as they did?'

She stared at him. Wherever could he be going with this? Her unease deepened. She would not have thought Sir George capable of drawing such conclusions. She bit her lip. Were these insights more likely to have come from Mr Woodward?

'I would think that most unlikely. They are still upset, of course, and fearful of you and this unwonted attention from such an important gentleman. That is all.'

'In that case, I cannot feel the education they are receiving here is having the desired effect. How long have they been with you?'

'Amy has been here about a year. Her sister followed her three months ago.

She is a little younger than most of our pupils, but since her sister was already here, it was felt — '

'Yes, I'm sure. But that is surely more than sufficient time for the shyest child to overcome the bad habits learned at home.'

Hannah gripped her fingers together. 'It is apparent you know very little about small girls, Sir George. Or even children in general. We work gently with the material we are given, but we cannot change them so swiftly. All children are different. And when you are a parent yourself, I am sure you will realise this.'

Hannah did not need to see the minister's warning glance. She recognised her mistake at once. She had touched a nerve and antagonised Sir George further. He glared at her. 'I had five brothers and sisters, Hannah. More than enough to gain an opinion. And all of us could conduct a conversation in company from a very young age indeed.'

'You had privileges and an upbringing unknown to most of my girls.'

'I felt the girls were telling the truth as they perceived it. Perhaps we may learn more from an older girl? But you have made some very relevant points, and Sir George and I will certainly keep them in mind as we proceed.'

Sir George nodded, seemingly mollified, and waved a hand for Hannah to continue. In the sanctuary of the corridor she shook her head, thinking how out of his depth he was. He obviously wanted nothing more than to have this odious business over and done and a conclusion reached in order to return to his idle, self-centred pursuits of pleasure. Yet circumstances were working against him, and the end seemed more distant at every turn.

She wished she could understand Mr Woodward as easily. Why had he hardly looked at her since his return? Before he left, she had felt certain of his support. Having stayed away longer than she had expected, now he seemed to be allying himself with Sir George.

But Sir George was only performing his legal duties. She must not resent that, as she needed to discover who had done this even more urgently than he did. If she could not always approve of his manner and methods, so be it. Occasionally, she remembered, he had shown compassion when dealing with sudden death. That servant girl at the hall who had taken her own life, for instance. Everyone in the village knew of it, and yet somehow Sir George had reached a verdict of accidental death, to the gratitude of the grieving family.

That had happened some years ago, before Sir George's marriage; but maybe he could still be compassionate. No — what was she thinking? Was she hoping he would conceal the facts, to enable the school to continue? She must not allow herself to hope for that. They must have the truth, whether the school survived this disaster or not. The offender must be brought to justice.

She stopped in front of the classroom

door, knowing she must face up to the possibility of the school not surviving. She clenched her hands together to stifle her distress. What about Margaret? The school had been set up with her in mind. She could never seek a post as a governess or companion.

Don't be foolish, she told herself. You are overreacting. The solution is plain, whether you like it or not. There is no husband in prospect for either of us, and no one likely to take Margaret on with myself, which is what they would have to do. Poor Margaret could unwittingly disrupt the most orderly household, and that is not what gentlemen require.

No, they must sell the house and purchase something much smaller, hoping the sale would provide a reasonable income for the rest of their lives. When this had been suggested after their father died, Margaret had been very distressed at the prospect, screaming and crying; but this time there would be no alternative. Hannah would have to make her understand.

'Are you all right, Miss Hannah?' Millie was beside her.

Hannah realised she was struggling to contain tears. 'Indeed, yes. I am merely gathering my thoughts.' She managed a weak smile.

'It's just that Mrs Copley sent me to ask whether the gentlemen will be wanting to see us, as you said; only there's the luncheon to prepare, miss.'

'Yes, of course. Proceed as usual, and we will manage the interviews around lunch. I expect both the minister and Sir George will be eating here. Wait a moment and I will find out.' She opened the classroom door. 'Alice, could you come with me a moment, please? Hush now, girls.' The wave of whispers and murmurs subsided. 'Here is Alice, gentlemen. One of my sensible girls. And can I tell Joan Copley that you will share a simple lunch?' Cold meat and pickles, but that would suffice.

'Yes, yes,' Sir George said quickly. 'Now may we continue?'

Alice's response was more confident than those of Lucy and Amy, even though at twelve she was next in age and also one of the younger girls. At first, she seemed equally unable to proffer anything of use. She had slept as soon as her head touched the pillow and only awoken to Lavinia's screams. Sir George sighed, seemingly ready to dismiss her.

'Wait,' Hannah said. 'Were you surprised to see Lavinia in your room, Alice?'

'Oh, no. She and Violet were often talking to each other when we were going to sleep. Sometimes in her room and sometimes in ours.'

'And last night?'

'No, not last night. They weren't speaking.'

There had been a disagreement between them? Hannah shook her head, annoyed with herself. Maybe there had been less chatter between the two older girls of late; but as this meant their duties were performed more easily and efficiently than usual, she had not troubled to worry about it. Yet again she had been distracted by the arrangements for the dinner party; a wasted effort, as there seemed little chance of gaining recommendations now.

And no, Alice had not heard heavy, hurrying footsteps or a man's voice. Hannah wished Sir George would frame his questions with a little more discretion; though this was unreasonable, she knew, as how else was he to gain the information they needed? But Alice was shaking her head, while her brows were almost rising to meet her mouse brown hairline. If there had been gossip and speculation before, now it would be running at fever pitch.

This showed how sound Hannah's instincts had been, to insist on accompanying the girls back to their classrooms where they would get on with their work. Once they compared accounts of Sir George's questioning and knew what he wanted, fevered imaginations would be producing any number of male intruders. She hoped Lavinia had been certain of her facts and not merely speculating. But it was done now; Sir George had seized on her account and was taking it seriously.

Hannah glanced down at Alice and was not reassured. The girl was fit to burst with importance. She would want to communicate what she had learned, and Margaret would be unable to prevent her. Margaret had good basic teaching capabilities when imparting certain skills, but maintaining discipline in the face of disruption was not among these. Hannah had always made a point of entering her classes at intervals to ensure all was well — as, usually, it was. Matters had improved since Violet and Lavinia had been enlisted to assist. And in the dormitories also; although of course Hannah had made a point of checking those too. Until last night. She pushed the critical thought away. Self-reproach would serve no useful purpose.

Hannah called Sophie, a placid child without an ounce of imagination; and Jenny Lee, the smallest, although older than Amy. Best to get this over as soon as possible.

Sophie considered each question with a determined frown, but had heard nothing. Jenny merely shook her head, wide-eyed. After the experience with Lucy and Amy, it seemed Sir George was happy to ignore her. Hannah was ushering them to the door when Sophie paused, saying, 'But I had a bad dream. I only remembered afterwards. A tall dark figure in a cloak was bending over me, and I opened my eyes and couldn't see a face, and it put a finger to where it should have had a face all in shadow, and then turned to Violet's bed.'

'We do not need dreams,' Sir George said in quite a kindly tone, 'interesting and fearsome although this must have been.'

But he did not know Sophie's character as Hannah did. She became aware Mr Woodward was staring at her, his eyes narrowed. He must be thinking as she was — what if this had not been a dream? If Sophie, drowsy with sleep, had mistaken reality for a nightmare?

Hannah shook her head. Futile questioning would only upset the little girl, for how was she to tell? It was difficult enough for an adult always to know the difference between dream and reality. She said nothing. Perhaps it was as well that Sir George seemed ready to ignore Sophie's fantasies. She and Jenny were ushered away with a brief word of praise and replaced by Emma, small and sensible, and Ellie, who had improved so much that Hannah regarded her with pride. Both had nothing to add and now came the turn of Mary Grey, the next oldest after Lavinia.

Hannah welcomed Mary's arrival almost with relief. This was an exemplary pupil who would deal well with responsibility. She stared calmly into Sir George's face with a straight gaze. Her answers were clear. No need here for Sir George to criticise the way she replied. Hannah's relief would be short-lived, however.

Yes, Mary had slept as usual. However, Lavinia had come in as she so often did for an exchange with her friend.

'With Violet?'

'Yes.'

'Was there not some disagreement between them?'

'There had been, but they made it up that very evening because they wanted to talk to each other about Miss Hannah's dinner. They were wondering why they could not have been included, since as older pupils, and teachers even, it would have been suitable for them to attend. But Violet said, 'Oh, no. They would be throwing their own chances away, she and Miss Margaret. You do not invite youth and beauty to provide rivalry, do you?' '

Hannah was aware of the colour rising through her throat and heating her face. 'Mary, this is gossip.'

'I am sorry, Miss Hannah. I know

Violet was gossiping, but that is what she said.'

'Of course.' Hannah tried to respond with suitable dignity. Maybe she was imagining a wave of compassion from the minister. She did not want pity, particularly not his. Surely he did not think there was any truth in Violet's innuendos? She wanted to stand up and deny them; to leap up and shout out, 'I am not on the catch for a husband. I am happy and self-sufficient in my own independence.' But she had already discovered that in Margaret's case, this would not be true. And no doubt Hannah would inevitably be painted with the same colour.

Dignity and plausibility lay in silence, however. Now her mind had wandered shamefully; and Sir George, looking pleased, as well he might, had moved on to the remainder of the evening. 'Are you a sound sleeper?'

'Yes, sir.'

'If one of the teachers enters the room, do you always hear them?'

'Sometimes I do.'

'And last night?'

'After Lavinia left, I went to sleep.'

Hannah said, 'Thank you, Mary.' And as Sir George nodded a dismissal, 'Shall we continue?'

'Oh, bring the rest in together. Surely there cannot be many more? I could welcome this light luncheon you mentioned.'

'Certainly, Sir George.' Hannah rose as the door burst open.

'I demand to know what is happening.' Margaret's voice was harsh. 'Am I to be ignored for the whole of the day?'

'Margaret! This is not the time — '

'*When* is it the time for me to be heard? I am pushed away on the excuse of caring for the girls when no care is required, because Lavinia could sit at the desk and keep order just as well. While you are closeted here . . . '

Oh no, not more of this. Hannah told Mary to make her own way to the classroom and took Margaret's arms gently but firmly. 'I am at fault. I should have kept you informed. Indeed, I was about to come and discuss all that has happened with you. Your opinion is always valued. Come now.'

'No,' Sir George said. 'We are obviously to interview Miss Margaret. Why not now, when all she may wish to share with us will be uppermost in her mind? Let your sister speak, please.'

6

Hannah indicated her own chair and Margaret sat down.

'You would do far better asking *me* what goes on in this school, Sir George. My sister believes herself to be in charge, but she has no idea, thinking herself so superior to poor, dear Margaret — but that is exactly why the girls do not trouble to hide their secrets from me. Poor Margaret — she won't know, she won't understand. They see Hannah coming and are silent, but they see me and their talk lingers just that little too long while they finish what they are saying, or nodding and winking. I pick things up, you see. A drib here, a drab there, and I end up better informed than anyone. Certainly more so than the lofty Miss Hannah here; for as soon as they hear the rustle of her gown or the tap of her keys, they are mum straightaway.' She made a gesture across her mouth with one hand, as if wiping a slate clean.

Hannah began to recover from the effect of the torrent of words. Even Sir George, who knew Margaret well, seemed bemused, while Mr Woodward sat as if stunned. She placed a hand on her sister's arm. 'Margaret!' she said sharply. 'You must wait for Sir George's questions.'

'Ah, you wish me to be silent. You are fearful of what I know that may harm the reputation of your precious school.'

'Not at all.' Little rivulets of alarm were pricking at the nape of Hannah's neck. 'Why should I? There is nothing to know.'

'So you say, so prim and proper. I am sure *you* know more than you admit. You want the school to carry on for years, and you wish to grow old here, but I see your plan; don't think I do not. In founding this school, you have laid a trap for us. We are seen as aging spinsters and objects of pity. Even our very rare dinner parties are attended from politeness or not at all; turned down with some flimsy excuse. I cannot blame Lady Foxcroft in the slightest, for it is apparent she would have better things to do.'

'Margaret! That is enough. Please.' Hannah's grip on her sister's arm tightened still more. To her shame, she was giving in to anger. After all her good intentions and promises to Father too — but always Margaret managed to get under her skin and say the worst possible things.

At last Sir George was responding. 'I think we should keep to specific answers concerning the matter in hand, Margaret.' He smiled kindly. 'When did you last see Violet?'

'Oh.' Margaret stared about her as if recovering from a trance, her shoulders slumping. 'It was an unusual evening. I should have overseen the children's preparations for bed and checked once or twice that both Lavinia and Violet were performing their duties. I'm entrusted to do that much, you see. Do not think Hannah bypasses me entirely.'

'And that evening?'

'Let me see . . . it was after we spoke on the stairs; that was earlier. I remember saying, 'You will be able to perform your customary duties alone this evening, I hope. I will be fully occupied, you know.' And she said, 'Oh, I believe I shall manage.' She had an insolent look at times. She thought I wouldn't notice, but I did. I was biding my time. 'You will get your comeuppance one day, Miss Violet,' I told myself. Hannah never noticed it of course. Violet would never dare be insolent to her.' Her face crumpled. 'Oh, dear. It has happened, hasn't it? Violet *has* got her comeuppance, so maybe someone else thought she deserved it too. But although she was annoying, it would not warrant murder . . .'

'Who spoke of murder?' Sir George's voice was very soft.

Hannah felt the blood drain from her

face. Surely he would not suspect Margaret? She so often spoke unwisely; everyone knew they could not take everything she said seriously.

Margaret was not worried. 'Sir George, this is a school full of girls. It is impossible here to keep the most secret fact hidden. There is never a door without someone listening behind it. Once a fact is known to one, it is known to all. You would be surprised at how quickly knowledge can spread.'

Sir George shifted in his chair. 'Knowledge? Surely you mean rumour and speculation.'

'That too, naturally. The false is always mixed in with the true.'

Hannah closed her eyes. It was not a pleasant picture Margaret had described, but at least this would divert suspicion from the rash statements she had made. In her relief, Hannah did not realise how Margaret was continuing. 'And Violet of course was a mistress of the collection and distribution of secrets. She had a little system of payments too. You would hardly believe how cleverly she managed it. Favours rendered and returned.'

Even Sir George now seemed at a loss for words. It was Mr Woodward who said, 'What kind of favours?'

'Oh, work could be passed that was not of a high standard; pages could be accepted as learned off when they were not. And in return . . . ' She leaned forward, speaking quietly. ' . . . the girls would not see or hear.'

Hannah could be silent no longer. 'Surely, Sir George, you cannot wish to accept this as evidence? I cannot see how this is helpful to us. You know Margaret, have done so for years, so you know how she is well-meaning but says whatever enters her head.'

'And what else would I do? What does everyone do?' Margaret protested.

'Of course,' Sir George said quickly. 'As you say, I know Margaret of old. I am sure we need not concern ourselves with any of this.'

The minister said quietly, 'See or hear what, Margaret?'

Margaret also lowered her voice. 'Comings and goings. Doors conveniently left unlocked. No one noticing a time of return.'

The minister said again, 'Who was coming and going? And where?'

Sir George said, 'This is hardly necessary, Woodward.'

'Oh, but I wish to speak,' Margaret cried. 'I can answer the questions. I wish to help with this enquiry. It was Violet, mainly. Well, entirely, I think. I would hesitate to involve Lavinia, though she knew of it, of course. She and Violet were as thick as thieves. An apt comparison, don't you think? Creeping about like thieves in the night. And Violet would let herself out of the side door as a matter of habit.'

Mr Woodward nodded. 'To go where?'

'Who can tell? Maybe Lavinia knows — but maybe not. Violet knew when to keep her secrets.'

Hannah could keep silent no longer. 'Margaret, if this was going on, why did

121

you not come to me?'

'Ah, you have all the power and I am of no account. I wanted to prove you wrong. This was a power *I* had. Something I knew and you did not. And I *was* intending to do something about it. I kept thinking, just a little more evidence and then Hannah cannot dismiss me as a fool and take all the credit for the discovery herself.'

Hannah shook her head. 'Credit? That would have been the last thing to concern me. Not when a pupil was putting herself at risk.'

Sir George said quickly, 'And if doors were left unlocked, how of intruders coming in? Lavinia told me she heard a man's heavy footsteps.'

'No. There were no intruders, not to my knowledge. Violet never went so far. For all her faults, she did care for the children. She would not have put *them* at such risk. And as for a man's footsteps — I am surprised you are seeking intruders, Sir George, when you might well look within the walls of

122

the school. What about the doctor and the minister here? Have you asked them?'

Sir George straightened. 'It is not for you to suggest what lines of enquiry I follow. Thank you, that will be all, Miss Margaret.'

'All? Already? But I have not told you the half of it.'

'I think you have told me all I wish to know. More than enough. Be assured, I will speak to you at a later date if the need arises.'

Margaret turned to Hannah, who nodded encouragingly, holding her breath. 'Thank you, Margaret. You have been very helpful, I'm sure.'

The minister rose. 'May I escort you back to the classroom, or wherever you may wish to go?'

Margaret simpered. 'Indeed, Reverend. You are very good.' As they reached the door, she turned to give Hannah a look of triumph.

Hannah was all too aware that Sir George had seen the exchange; she nodded as if in recognition. What else could she do? Oh, this would happen now, when Margaret had seemed so much better over the last couple of years. Hannah had been so certain Margaret had settled to their new life with a degree of contentment. *It seems I was mistaken. I had no idea she regretted the lack of a husband and a home life so much. I had no idea about a great many things, as she has made perfectly plain.*

Hannah realised Sir George was regarding her thoughtfully, as if waiting for her to speak. Trying to keep her voice steady, she said, 'I can only apologise.'

'None needed. You forget, I have known Margaret and her problems from childhood.'

'Of course. So you will be able to accept that much of what she says is merely born of a feverish and overactive imagination.'

'Maybe so.' He paused. 'But *you* must accept I cannot dismiss her testimony as a whole. She has made certain allegations that must be investigated thoroughly.'

'What? But surely you cannot take her account seriously.'

'I cannot afford *not* to do so.'

Hannah put a hand to her forehead, trying to remember exactly what Margaret had said. 'What in particular? Which parts do you feel you must take seriously?'

'I am afraid I am unable to share my thoughts on this. In my official position, it would not be appropriate, you understand.'

'But surely, in these particular circumstances . . . '

'No. Others may well consider I have allowed you to take part in these investigations too much already. Now I must be left to follow my own directions and form my own opinions. You, Hannah, are amongst the interviewees and witnesses, nothing more. You cannot take the role of adviser.'

She said sharply, 'And the minister?

Is he not equally a witness?'

Woodward's voice came from the doorway. 'Indeed I am.' He smiled. 'But I would like to offer myself as a professional observer, if you would find that useful, Sir George. And I believe where the children are concerned, and an opinion is needed, Miss Brockley's presence would be most useful.'

Hannah's thoughts were in turmoil. Was this the time for her to speak out about the footprints? If she did not, she would be colluding in his guilt, if such it was. But she had envisaged having more time to think about this, to decide upon her approach and ask him discreetly when they were alone. If she had done so, however, any response he made would not be witnessed by anyone else. He could respond to her as he chose. No, she must speak out now.

They were settling back into their original seats. Whatever was she going to say? Should she confront him now? Yes, she must. Hannah said, 'I wondered whether Mr Woodward might have something to add to his account?'

Both men stared at her. Sir George was frowning, but to her faint surprise, Mr Woodward nodded. 'Certainly. What do you wish to ask me?'

'Afterwards, when everyone else had gone back to their beds, did you not examine the building for signs of intruders?'

Woodward nodded solemnly. 'I did.'

'And did you find anything? Were the doors and windows secured?'

'Yes, they were.'

'The snow,' Hannah said, her throat dry. 'Did we not examine the snow for footprints?'

'We did. We saw none from the upper windows, Sir George. Hannah will corroborate this.'

'You were to examine the ground outside more closely.' Hannah could hardly form the words.

'Thank you. I will deal with the questioning if you please.' Sir George was becoming irritable.

'As you will have seen as you arrived,

Sir George,' Mr Woodward said, 'there are no footprints there. The snow is still plainly visible.'

A leaden feeling planted itself below Hannah's breastbone. She realised how much she liked Mr Woodward and had not wanted him to lie. He was destroying her trust with every word he uttered. He must surely have a plausible explanation. She was formulating another question, and so much depended on his answer. How would she feel about him from this moment on?

He was staring into a space somewhere between her and Sir George. *Look at me. Please. Surely you cannot look straight at me and lie? And if you do, what reason would you have for lying?* She said, 'There are no prints there now, yes. But what if someone . . . deliberately . . . destroyed them?'

He turned at last and looked directly at her. She could not read the look on his face. Regret? Sadness? He said, 'Sir George, may I speak to you privately?'

'Well, of course,' Sir George said with

128

obvious irritation. 'It was only at your own request Miss Hannah was included at all. Hannah, if you please?'

Somehow, unwillingly, but without anyone's hand upon her, she found herself out in the corridor. She shook her arms, feeling as if she had been bundled out. What could Mr Woodward have to say to Sir George that he did not wish her to hear? At least he had not lied to her. She must be thankful for that, she supposed. But would he tell Sir George the truth?

Well, she could not stand out here doing nothing. As Margaret had pointed out, her place was with the children.

'Oh, Miss Hannah!' Millie was trotting towards her, breathing quickly.

'Slowly, slowly,' Hannah said automatically. 'Yes, Sir George and Reverend Woodward are almost ready for luncheon. They will only be a matter of minutes.'

'No, miss. I mean, yes. But it's Mrs Kershaw now. She's come back, wanting a word with you. Something to do with the laying out. Something she still had to see to. So I showed her upstairs.'

'Certainly. I shall come at once.'

'She's in the room with the . . . with Violet.' Millie lowered her voice. 'I said I'd see if you were free, though I didn't think you would be.'

Hannah frowned as she walked up the stairs, without haste. She did not recall being asked for when their father had died and his poor stricken body had been carried back here. Though that had been such a devastating time, and with Margaret's hysterics to see to; her memories of those days were unclear.

She opened the door to the dormitory and realised Millie was still behind her, face alive with interest. 'Thank you, Millie.' Hannah smiled. The maid's reaction told her that her instincts had been correct. She waited for Millie to hurry away before saying, 'Mrs Kershaw? You wished to speak to me?'

The old woman was standing beside the fruits of her labours. She gestured to the girl's body and Hannah nodded her approval. 'Yes, this is excellent. She looks completely at peace. I thought so when I looked at her earlier.' Her hands were folded, eyes closed, hair gleaming in the light of a solitary reverential candle.

'I'm glad of your approval, miss. Always a sad task with one so young.' Mrs Kershaw looked suitably sad, but her fingers were twitching with unease.

Hannah wondered suddenly whether Mrs Kershaw had wished to mention the head wound. 'Do not be afraid to speak. Were there any problems in particular that you wished to mention to me?'

'Not as such.' Mrs Kershaw hesitated. 'It's just that I feel someone should know, considering the circumstances. Don't misunderstand me, I know how to be discreet, none better. I can't help but hold many secrets, being in my position. But with Sir George asking questions, I didn't know what to do; whether to approach him. Better, I thought, to tell you. You'll know what must be done.'

'Tell me what?'

'This girl, Violet, was with child. There can be no mistake.'

7

Hannah went to her small private bedroom in a daze. She needed to be alone; to think. 'I understand,' she had said to Mrs Kershaw. 'Thank you. I shall have to consider this.' And yes, she understood more than she wanted to.

She must have seemed silent and preoccupied through luncheon, and as both Sir George and Mr Woodward finally left. For the rest of the day, her thoughts kept returning to this unwelcome news. How she had put a hand to her face at the shock of it. How Mrs Kershaw had apologised for broaching this sensitive subject with herself, a single lady, and Hannah had striven to soothe her doubts, assuring her she had acted in an entirely proper way.

What was to be done now? Should she entrust Sir George with this information? What would happen if it should be broadcast to everyone at the inevitable inquest? For surely there would have to be one.

If this distressing news had nothing to do with Violet's death, there was no need to tell him. However, it might have everything to do with it. Without knowing who had been responsible for Violet's condition, it would be impossible to make a decision.

How would Violet's parents respond to this? She had now sent a message with the tragic news to the girl's father but could not tell how he would react. Violet had been brought to the school when her father married again. Frequently a widower would remarry purely to find a new mother for his children — but sometimes the new spouse did not care to have these reminders of past happiness about her.

When Hannah had first met Violet's father, his farewell to his daughter had seemed brief and uncaring. But surely he would care about the manner of her death? She must wait for his response, without judging him in advance.

Also, she must confront Mr Woodward. What were the private matters he had imparted to Sir George? She was finding herself drawn to certain unwelcome conclusions. The footprints in the snow had not been those of an intruder; they were too small and slender for that. They must be Violet's; possibly going to a meeting with her lover. That would corroborate Margaret's account also.

Hannah winced, but there could be no denying it. Perhaps Violet had told this man of her condition and he had reacted with anger. Enough to kill her? She felt a chill creep down her back. If so, what better reason could there be for destroying the evidence of Violet's nocturnal wanderings?

It all pointed to the minister. Had he been romantically and unsuitably entangled with Violet — and murdered her? Hannah moaned a little, pushing a fist into her mouth. How could she have been so mistaken about him? She sat for some time, heedless of who might need her, staring into the empty grate before reason slowly reasserted itself.

Why should Violet leave the school to meet Mr Woodward when he was within the building already? To avoid being seen, perhaps. But they would be even more likely to be seen from the windows. It would take only a restless pupil or a mistress looking out to discover them. From the corridor, however, it would need only a swift glance in both directions to enter any empty room one chose, unseen.

She was suddenly almost overwhelmed by an intense feeling of weariness. She wished from the bottom of her heart she had not looked from the east window and seen that sight. But she had. *Tell Sir George*, her inner voice urged. *Tell him about Mr Woodward, tell him Mrs Kershaw's tale and let him disentangle it all. Through status and inheritance, he gained the official position and legal approval for this. Let him do it.*

She shifted uneasily. Although Sir George had already surprised her by the thoroughness of his investigation, there was no guarantee he would discover the truth. But he would discover a truth of sorts, and they would all have to abide by that. And now she realised she had been absent for far too long. She would have to tell Sir George. She went downstairs — and found Mr Woodward, just when she wanted to avoid him.

'Ah, Miss Hannah. Violet's father is here.'

'Already?' Hannah began a ridiculous and irrelevant calculation of the distance to Huddersfield and back, the time Tom might have taken to reach the house. As if that mattered, since Mr Scrimshaw was here, and before she had even half-begun to think what she would say to him.

'Millie has shown him into the study,' Mr Woodward said. 'So I volunteered to tell you, to prepare you a little.'

Hannah nodded. 'Thank you. That was most kind of you.' Again, events had been taken out of her hands. Wherever he might be at fault, it was unfair to blame the minister for the speed of Mr Scrimshaw's arrival, and her thoughts must now be entirely for Violet's father and his loss.

Mr Scrimshaw was staring before him, his face unreadable. Hannah took a breath and straightened her shoulders. 'Mr Scrimshaw, I am so very sorry.'

The man shook his head. 'The minister here has told me of what has occurred.'

'Has he?' Hannah's suspicions loomed between them and could not be dispersed.

Mr Scrimshaw said stiffly, 'I wish only to take her home. This is what I hoped — and my sorrowing wife also. But the minister tells me we must wait for an inquest. An inquest? Why must this be?'

'I am afraid that is so,' Hannah said

carefully. 'It will be to establish the cause of her death.'

'Why is that needful? Has the body not been viewed by a doctor? Young girls are always subject to sudden illnesses and weakness. It happens all the time. I see no need for any legal nonsense.'

'There are circumstances ... ' Hannah stopped, then began again. 'It seems the cause of death is not straightforward.'

He stepped forward, bringing his face close to hers. 'Not straightforward? Miss Brockley, I left my child in your care, and paid fees per quarter for so doing. This is not what I wish to hear.'

'Your feelings do you credit,' the minister said. 'And we are all sorry for the delay at your time of such grief. But I know Sir George, as the magistrate, wants the proceedings to occur as speedily as possible. Miss Brockley, I have told Mr Scrimshaw he is welcome to stay with me until we know what is to happen.'

'I see. Thank you.' This was not something she had thought of — and hardly necessary, surely? His home was hardly more than a few miles away.

'I am grateful, of course.' Mr Scrimshaw bowed. He did not seem grateful.

Hannah said, 'You will want to see your daughter?'

'Ah, yes. I suppose so.'

Again Mr Woodward followed. Hannah did not object. Whatever the truth of what had happened, the minister seemed to have a gift for smoothing awkward moments with his apt comments. As she had half-suspected, Mr Scrimshaw's time with his daughter's body proved somewhat perfunctory. Hannah said, 'You are most welcome to sit with her.'

He frowned. 'Sit with her?'

'In quiet reflection?'

'Hah! It seems to me that my daughter was the one who should have benefited from reflection. She was always flighty and given to undesirable impulses. I had hoped that her stay here would encourage her into a steadier and more thoughtful frame of mind. And now she has met her death in a way requiring an inquest. This is not at all satisfactory.'

Hannah sighed. 'We were pleased with Violet's progress here. She had a gift for teaching and could have eventually been offered a permanent post with us. With your agreement, of course.' Colour entered her face. Obviously, with a child, everything would have been different. Hannah did not know what their next steps might have been. A very different message would have been sent to Violet's father. She shuddered to think how that would have been received.

'Come, Scrimshaw,' Woodward said. 'Perhaps you might welcome a quiet discussion with myself on this sad occasion. I can take you through the circumstances as we know them. You could join me in prayer in my chapel. And I can show you where you will be welcome to stay at the manse.'

'I suppose that will have to suffice.' Mr Scrimshaw frowned at Hannah. 'For now.'

The Reverend Woodward took his arm to lead him gently from the landing, smiling reassuringly at Hannah behind his back. She suspected that Mr Woodward would encourage Scrimshaw to voice all his complaints against Hannah and the school and would then proceed to dismiss them, with tact and subtlety. Mr Scrimshaw would feel he had been granted a sympathetic ear, and that might indeed suffice. Suspecting his true feelings for poor Violet, and how the second wife was unlikely to wish any great fuss to be made about her stepdaughter, Hannah was hopeful of that.

While she was grateful to Mr Woodward, however, she still wished to speak to him alone and discover the truth, and not only about the footprints. She wanted to hint at what Mrs Kershaw had told her and watch his reaction. Once he had managed to calm

Mr Scrimshaw, she fully expected a swift return, if only to tell her that his tactics had been successful.

* * *

By the next afternoon, however, there was still no sign of him, or Mr Scrimshaw, or even Sir George. After all the activity of the day before, the place seemed unnaturally quiet and subdued. Lessons were proceeding as usual, but there was an underlying feeling of tension and unease. Hannah found herself listening for a knock at the front door and voices in the hall announcing an arrival. What was happening? To hold an inquest, would a coroner have to be informed? Nothing was certain.

At last, when her heart leapt in her breast as Amy Green dropped her slate, Hannah knew she could stand it no longer. She made a decision: if Mr Woodward would not come here, she would take the initiative and seek to surprise him. It was merely a fifteen-minute walk on the path across the fields and by now the snow was lying only in the shadow of the stone walls. The decision made, she was ready in minutes, giving herself no chance to think again.

Halfway along the path, she smiled wryly, realising her mistake. From here, she could easily see the windows of the manse. If Mr Woodward should be looking out, he might easily avoid her still, if he so chose.

Yes, the minister had indeed seen her coming; however, he opened the door to her himself. Now he was exclaiming at the dampness of her hem and her wet boots in this inclement weather. 'You only had to send to me, Miss Brockley, and I would have come to you.'

Hannah raised her brows. 'Really? But I would not wish to take you from your parochial duties any further. You have been too punctilious in your care of us already. Please do not fuss; I have had wet feet many times before and doubtless will do so again, and have never yet come to harm. My father always said wet soles were good for the soul.'

Woodward laughed. 'Did he?'

'He felt a little discomfort was of benefit to one's character and should be sought out whenever possible.'

'I am sure it may well be so. But rather a grim philosophy, perhaps.'

'No doubt that's why he diluted it with a joke. My father was by no means a grim and forbidding person.' This would not do. She had not intended to become sidetracked into discussing her father.

Into the awkward pause, Woodward said, 'Have you come to see Mr Scrimshaw? He is at present in the library. Poor man, this is a difficult time, just waiting for Sir George to tell us what will happen next. I do not know how best to advise him; whether he should go home to support his wife. It is not a good time to be alone.'

'Mrs Scrimshaw has her own children around her for comfort,' Hannah said. 'She is a woman of a strong and determined character and will have made her choice knowingly, I'm sure — and if she feels the lack of her husband, will send for him.'

'Yes, I'm sure you are right. You have the situation exactly. You will have met the lady?'

'No. But we have mutual acquaintances.' She smiled politely. 'You will soon discover everyone here has links to everyone else this side of Leeds.'

Woodward nodded. 'That's good. As a minister, one wishes to do the very best for those in one's care, but sometimes the best way is far from clear. The library is in here.' He was ushering her to a door on the left.

'No — wait, please. I have not come to speak to Mr Scrimshaw, although I will enquire briefly in a moment as to how he does. I have come to see you. Is there somewhere we may be more private?'

146

'Oh, that I can offer you in abundance. I rattle around in this vast house like a pea in a bottle. I have three dining rooms and several studies.'

Hannah wondered whether the humour was now forced. Perhaps he was trying to emphasise the friendship between them, because he must surely suspect what she wanted to say. 'That's very convenient, then,' she said.

'Can I offer you some refreshment?'

'Later, perhaps.' Refreshment would mean an enforced pause while the housekeeper bustled in and out.

Woodward was opening a door to their right. 'At least there's a fire in here. I was preparing my current sermon.' He moved a chair nearer the fire for her. Hannah had a sudden illogical dread of how those capable hands might feel around her throat. She shuddered. She must be careful. If Mr Woodward should be the murderer, had she foolishly placed herself in danger?

Nonsense! Mr Scrimshaw and the housekeeper were mere yards away.

They would both hear any call for help. And yet, Violet had died with five other girls present in the same room. So why had Hannah not taken her information and suspicions to Sir George? But she knew why. Because she liked Mr Woodward and wanted him to proffer a plausible explanation. The unwanted thought crept in: more than liked?

Mr Woodward sat down facing her. 'You are troubled; I can see that.' The smile had been wiped away. The blue eyes were serious. 'I know why you have come. I have to apologise. My behaviour must seem inexplicable.'

'Oh?'

'You saw me that night. From the upper window.'

She stared at him. She had not expected him to admit it so easily.

'When I was dealing with the footprints in the snow. Violet's footprints, I was certain of it.' He nodded. 'I see it in your face. I suspected as much at the time, when you asked whether I had been out. What must you be thinking of me?'

'I was shocked and confused. Surely your actions were most unwise?'

'I know. I acted precipitately. That was the decision I took.' He shrugged. 'Rightly or wrongly. I saw the prints, small and slender, and drew a swift and inevitable conclusion. To me, they seemed to point to — something undesirable in Violet's character which I thought could only damage you and the school if it became widely known.'

'I know.' Hannah alone had heard Mrs Kershaw's information; the prints had to be evidence of Violet's misdemeanours. 'All the same, I wish you had not done it.' *My fault*, she thought. *As Mr Scrimshaw said, Violet was given into my charge.* She said aloud, 'I should have cared for her better. I should have foreseen this and prevented it.'

'You were not to know.'

'It was my duty to know. To be fully aware of any faults in the girls and young women in my care and strive to alter their characters.'

'If Violet did not want you to know, there was no reason you should. It seems she deceived us all. And I too must confess my guilt. To protect you and your sister, I erased the footprints, wilfully destroying valuable evidence. It was a whim, an impulse. To do it at all, I had to act quickly.'

'And does Sir George know of this?'

'Sir George? Yes, he does now.'

She nodded, relieved. 'But why speak to him in private, when you are willing to tell me of it?'

'I considered my actions fully last night. As things stood, I came to the conclusion that what Sir George did with the information would be his decision, for good or ill. But if I tell him you also know, that may affect his choice.'

'What do you mean? You are not suggesting . . . ' The conversation seemed to be entering unknown waters.

He said, too quickly, 'No, I am not intending any criticism of Sir George.

Do not even say it. We shall have to wait and see.'

Hannah found Mr Woodward's remark disconcerting. Would Sir George be likely to take the easier course? Would he take steps to ensure these aspects of the evidence did not come to light? And what of herself — was she not doing the same thing? She now held Mrs Kershaw's evidence in trust; she had to make the decision as to what should be done with that knowledge. But she had not hurried away to Sir George to tell him of it. She sighed. She was also at fault, and could not condemn Mr Woodward.

Woodward was watching her silently, waiting while she disentangled her thoughts. She gave a long sigh. 'I see,' she said. But she did not. She would like to be as open with the minister as possible, as he had seemed to be with her. Looking into those clear, steady blue eyes, how could anyone mistrust him? She shook herself a little. Blue eyes were merely a gift of nature and no guarantee of truthfulness. Too many women were so easily misled by laughing eyes and a veneer of sincerity. But she would not be, never again. She had been all too easily convinced by Sir George in those far-off days when he had attempted to charm her.

How should she answer the minister? She rehearsed the words silently. *I would like to believe you, Reverend Woodward, but I can't. I have no proof of what you tell me. Until we know who killed Violet. I cannot trust anyone.* No — better to give the impression that she did believe him.

'I am glad the explanation was so simple,' she said. 'That is a profound relief to me. My father always said I was foolishly capable of seeking out demons of complexity where none existed.' She smiled. Did her words sound convincing?

Woodward's features relaxed. 'That's good. I am pleased we have been able to talk in this way. I felt I was in danger of losing your friendship, and I would not want that.'

Hannah rose, her legs unsteady. 'I would not wish that either. But I can assure you that our friendship has never been in danger.' Why did she feel so shaky? A further relief at Woodward's acceptance of what she had just said? The way his eyes gained warmth as he spoke of friendship? Against her will, Hannah felt a spark igniting within her that she had thought never to feel again. But she must not allow it, she told herself. Those foolish emotions were for girls like Violet, rather than staid maiden ladies in their late twenties.

She left with a considered lack of haste, not wanting to betray her feelings, and remembering to exchange a few sympathetic words with Mr Scrimshaw on the way out, although whether he appreciated the courtesy was doubtful. Only when out in the cold, piercing air were her thoughts stilled a little. Did Woodward believe her little charade? Or was he still playing his own game, not one jot deceived by hers — and if so, what game *was* he playing?

From the corner of her eye, she caught a glimpse of something on the horizon: the motionless silhouette of a horse and rider. Almost as if watching her. She turned her head. There was no one there now. She must have imagined it.

Somewhere in this very neighbourhood, there was someone capable of murder. Had she been wise to come out here alone, telling no one where she had gone? It could so easily appear that she had slipped on the remaining patches of ice, hitting her head as she fell, and no one would think anything of it. She pulled her cloak around her and looked over her shoulder as she hurried back.

8

Hannah arrived safely at her own door almost with a feeling of shame; no one had waylaid her on the path as she had foolishly imagined they might.

She must once again regard the school as her home and her refuge. Violet's death had been a tragic mischance, doubtless never to be solved in spite of Sir George's efforts. And whoever had been the culprit, there was no further danger, because that situation would never occur here again. Hannah would see to that.

She must conquer her inevitable feelings of dread and unease. For now, she must concentrate on ensuring the best of care for her pupils, and hope they would recover from the unsettling events of this week as soon as possible. Sadly, many families had to endure child mortality. This was accepted.

Children were resilient, as they had to be. So she would endeavour to restore the school routine as soon as possible.

Hannah opened the front door and walked in to a tumult of noise and confusion. The girls from both class-rooms were no longer diligently at their desks, but milling about in the hall. At the centre of the storm were Millie and Lavinia; Lavinia seemed to be scream-ing urgent questions and Millie was close to tears, shaking her head with her hand over her ears.

Hannah knew she must take control. She filled her lungs with air and cried, 'Silence! All of you,' in a voice she had never before used since the school began. They all turned to stare at her, frozen like small statues in a children's game. One or two of the smallest began to cry. The reassuring hugs must come later; for now she must handle this crisis, whatever it was.

Lavinia was temporarily stilled but she was already drawing breath to direct her onslaught at Hannah. Hannah raised a hand. 'No, Lavinia. You may tell me — but calmly. And briefly, please.'

Lavinia clasped her hands together. 'Thank goodness you've come back, Miss Hannah. When no one knew where you were, we didn't know what to do.'

'Lavinia, what is the matter?' Hannah was now speaking very quietly. 'Take a deep breath.'

At last, Lavinia obeyed. 'I hardly know how to tell you. It's Miss Margaret. She's disappeared.'

Hannah stared at her. She wanted to say, 'What nonsense. What do you mean?' But that would only result in a further bout of noise and disorder. Instead she said, 'Let us all calm ourselves. In a moment you may tell me all about it. I am sure there will be some simple explanation. But for now, girls, will you return to your desks, please.'

Lavinia said sulkily, 'I have been trying to run both classes alone. Miss Margaret should have been taking today's spellings, and I was trying to do my lesson. And Miss Hoyle is nowhere to be seen.'

'Girls, all of you go and take your primers and copy the very first page in your most beautiful handwriting. I shall inspect them all, and the best will be displayed in my private study, to be seen by visitors.'

'It should have been arithmetic,' Lavinia muttered.

'As I produced the timetable, I am well aware of that. But for the moment, we shall forego both spelling and arithmetic in favour of our little competition.' Already some of the girls were walking quietly away, seemingly more cheerful at the prospect of having a clear instruction.

'Lavinia, come and speak to me in my study, please. This will be easily dealt with, I'm sure.' The confident tone was for the benefit of the last of the children as they left. Lavinia's sulky expression told Hannah the girl was far from convinced. Millie was still hovering in the background also, looking equally doubtful. 'I'll come and see you in a few minutes, Millie. Don't worry; I am sure none of this is your fault. Continue with your duties for now, if you please.' Millie hurried away, her face pink with relief.

Hannah said nothing more until the study door was closed behind them.

'Now, Lavinia, please sit down. My dear, I know you are very young and have had experiences thrust upon you that we all deplore. But if you are to become a successful pupil-teacher, you must realise that in front of the children, calm must be maintained at all costs. Their reactions and well-being must be paramount, whatever happens.' She raised a hand. 'No, wait. Do not tell me until you can speak quietly. A calm demeanour is essential at all times. And you may begin practising this ideal from this moment, please.'

She watched the expressions of frustration cross Lavinia's face. As she had thought, Lavinia had been almost enjoying the drama. A hard lesson, but one well learned. This was not easy for Hannah either, when she was desperate for information and felt anything but calm. At last, she was satisfied. 'Now, please tell me what has happened.'

There was the merest shakiness in Lavinia's voice. 'Miss Margaret has disappeared.'

'Yes, so I gather. Please elaborate.'

'She is nowhere to be found. I realised there was too much noise coming from the other classroom, and I didn't want to interfere with Miss Margaret's lesson; but at last with the hubbub rising, I went and she wasn't there. And then I sent Millie to look for her — thinking of her class, you see, just as you said. And Millie couldn't find her or you either, not in her room or anywhere. And Miss Hoyle is too ill to help.'

'I see.' Hannah nodded with a quiet dignity, although her thoughts were racing. 'I can quite understand why you were concerned, but I am sure there is nothing to worry about. As we all know,

Miss Margaret can be subject to sudden whims and fancies.' The excuses slid easily from her tongue. She hardly had to think about them; for years she had been finding plausible reasons to try and explain Margaret's actions, to protect her.

Perhaps, yet again, it was all her fault. Margaret had made it plain she did not feel Hannah was paying her enough attention. *But what else was I to do?* Hannah sighed. And yet she might as well have left Sir George and Mr Woodward to their own devices, for all the difference she had made. And in some way, Margaret had been neglected and harmed.

As soon as Margaret was found, Hannah would ensure that she made it up to her. After their father's death, her sister had been grief-stricken, but she had responded so sensibly to Hannah's suggestion of starting the school and had taken to the actual teaching so well. In many ways, she had seemed more mature. Parents bringing their children to the school often had no idea that Margaret was somewhat . . . different.

'First, I shall set further work for all the girls, to occupy them for another half hour,' Hannah said, 'and then I shall check the whole house myself, slowly and thoroughly.' As a child, Margaret would often run away and hide. That would be what had happened. The stress of Violet's death and the questioning had unnerved her, causing her to seek refuge in childish habits. That was easily dealt with. Hannah knew all her favourite hiding places — although Margaret would no longer be able to fit into the cubbyhole beneath the servants' stairs, or the back of the linen cupboard. Should she get the servants to help? They knew about the problem already, thanks to Lavinia and her hysterical outburst. But she rejected the idea at once. When found, Margaret would need the calm and reassurance only a loving sister could provide.

Hannah set out filled with optimism,

quashed as every possible hiding place was considered, visited and rejected. Every cupboard, the attics and cellars. Ah, the outbuildings. As children they had played with their dolls in the old tack room. That would be it.

She was convinced she had it right this time, only for the dull acceptance of failure once more when the old tack room was empty. When her grandfather had been alive, they had kept five horses, or so her father had told her. Now they had none, the last being sold when her father died. So many changes; so difficult for Margaret to cope with. And now the crisis of Violet's death. No wonder Margaret had run off to hide.

The search seemed to take a long time; longer than the half hour she had thought, and yet not long enough. All too soon, every possible place was exhausted. She had to accept what she should have suspected straightaway: Margaret had gone. She leaned against the splintering door. What to do next? Realising that someone was speaking to her, she looked up.

'Are you all right, Miss Hannah?'

'I beg your pardon? Oh, yes. I'm sorry, Tom.' She made a decision. It was unlikely that she would find Margaret by herself, and the luxury of calm reassurance was now lost to her. 'I'm searching for Miss Margaret. Could you look for her in the grounds?'

Tom Turley nodded and strode away.

Hannah's throat contracted. She could barely swallow. What if Margaret had become another victim? No, as a child, Margaret was always threatening to leave home when anything annoyed her, to seek more kindly care — but it was never meant. Never acted upon. So where was she?

Wait. Think this through. Calmly. Go back to Margaret's room and search with more thought and a different object in view. This would tell her whether Margaret had left deliberately or had been horridly waylaid and abducted. She flung open the cupboard in her sister's room and yes, Margaret had indeed taken some items of clothing. If she checked the attic, no doubt she would discover a carpet bag was missing also.

Her relief was short-lived. At least Margaret had gone of her own volition but there was no telling what might have happened to her once outside. Calm. That was becoming her watch-word. She leaned a hand against the bedrail, taking deep, soothing breaths, the other hand pressed to her heart.

No time for such melodramatics. Make use of the upper windows. She should have thought of that before, rather than sending Tom to cover the same ground. Yes, the pathway leading to the Manse was clearly visible — and empty. Also the way to the village. But by now, Margaret would have reached her destination wherever it might be.

Maybe Hannah had been too hasty in sending Tom off around the grounds. He must go to the village and ask if anyone had seen Margaret. No, better if she did that herself. There were too many directions to be covered, and she did not like to be away from the school for too long. Lavinia could not be trusted to keep control.

There was Miss Hoyle, of course. How easy it was to ignore her. Yes, she must be instructed to leave her sick bed, which seemed to be sought as a matter of convenience, and take up her duties. Also, there was Mary Grey — she could become a temporary pupil-teacher; and this, Hannah told herself, would be enough to maintain control.

It was unlikely that Margaret would have sought refuge with Miss Hoyle in her room, since she had taken one of her irrational dislikes to her. Or was it so irrational? Miss Hoyle had only been given the privilege of a room alone, on the top floor, to allow her to avoid the noise made by the girls. Hannah was sorry for her predicament, but she had taken her in to help with the girls, not to avoid them. She must harden her heart.

At least Miss Hoyle was up; although when Hannah entered, she sank back weakly in her chair, a handkerchief to her forehead. And when the problem was explained to her, she showed little sympathy. 'Most unfortunate, I am sure, but there is nothing I can do about it. I have not seen Margaret.'

'You are needed downstairs,' Hannah said crisply. 'I wish you to return to your teaching duties at once. I am sure walking about and the company of others will do you nothing but good.'

'I still feel so weak.'

'I am not going to discuss this. I have every sympathy for your afflictions, but now I have urgent need of you. The work is set. It is only a matter of keeping order so that your presence is felt.'

'As long as the girls do not speak loudly. It is those high piping voices I find so trying. They do chatter so.'

Hannah somehow managed to maintain her patience. 'Never fear, I shall issue the firmest instructions. There will be no chattering. Or piping either.' Margaret had been right. She had offered Miss Hoyle a refuge in her hour of need, but had hoped for at least a nominal contribution to the work of the school. Miss Hoyle, however, was all too happy to enjoy the privilege of doing very little.

'Oh, very well.'

And all this when Hannah's every nerve was quivering to continue with her search. But at last Miss Hoyle and Lavinia and a serious and wide-eyed Mary Grey were installed in the classrooms and further tasks set.

Hannah returned to the quiet sanctuary of her study. She needed to think. Had Margaret set out blindly, in anger, or had she some firm destination in mind? She must try and put herself in Margaret's place, try and think as she did and decide where she might have gone. Where might she seek refuge?

With any of their former pupils? Girls leaving tearfully had often issued invitations to other girls and even their teachers in the emotion of the moment. The girls often loved Margaret, although she frequently did not return their devotion.

No, think further back. To when their father had been alive and Margaret little more than a child. Of course, how simple it was. The solution was glaringly clear: Nanny Toft, their old nurse, as Miss Hoyle had been Sir George's. Margaret had been devoted to her. It was a bond of fondness and love never to be broken. Nanny Toft would have been welcome to stay here as long as she wished, but she had left reluctantly to care for an ailing sister living near Leeds. The Brockley sisters had both missed her, although she wrote frequently. She had understood Margaret well, dealing with her with a loving firmness and patience Hannah wished she could emulate.

Yes, this seemed more and more likely. Another wave of relief. And once there, Margaret would be safe. Hannah should have thought of that straight-away instead of searching the house so frantically. On the heels of the relief, however, came yet more doubts. If Margaret had gone there, would Nanny Toft not have sent word? Hannah would not rest until she knew, and whether Margaret had arrived safely. Should she send Tom to ask? But how long would that take? And if she was wrong, she might well need him here.

Who could she ask? Who could be trusted? At one time, Sir George would have been her first thought when needing help, but latterly his manner had not been encouraging. During his investigations, his demeanour had been stern. Obviously he thought Hannah at fault in some way, and she could only agree. Violet had been a vulnerable young woman in her care. There was no escaping that thought.

Perhaps the doctor would undertake the errand for her? Margaret had always liked him and would not be upset by his arrival. He had declared himself eager to be of use — while hastening away as quickly as possible. Yes, Hannah would surprise him by taking him up on his half-meant offer.

She heard the jangle of the bell at the front door and Millie's voice. 'The minister and Mr Scrimshaw, Miss.'

That was one destination she could discount, at any rate. If Margaret had gone to the Manse, Hannah would have met her as she returned.

Mr Woodward smiled as he shook her hand. 'I have brought Mr Scrimshaw to spend an hour or so with Violet, if that is acceptable to you?'

'Yes, of course. For as long as you wish.'

Mr Scrimshaw said, 'We decided any message about the inquest would necessarily be sent here first. I wished to waste no time. And I realise my wife would advise it. She is always aware of the proprieties. When I first arrived, I was overwhelmed with the shock.'

'I shall take you to her, of course.'

Mr Woodward hung back a little as

they left the room. 'You look tired. More so than when you left the Manse. Is something wrong?'

She found herself telling him when she had not intended to. The warmth and sympathy that was so customary in his calling, no doubt. And when he was so obviously wanting to be helpful, it was hard not to trust him. But whoever had killed Violet must have been skilled in deceit.

'Leeds?' he said immediately. 'Let me go. Please. If you will give me the direction, I can be on my way at once.'

'No, I cannot ask that of you. You have your duty with Mr Scrimshaw here. You have dealt with him so well and I am most grateful.'

'I believe he will prefer to be alone. For him there is strength in solitude.'

'Indeed,' Mr Scrimshaw said. 'You must go, if you are needed elsewhere. And I need no more of your Nonconformist sermonising either.'

Mr Woodward grinned at her. 'My talents are not always appreciated.

Don't worry, I shall not be away long, I shall borrow one of the doctor's horses; I do not even need to ask. A permanent and generous offer on his part, though generally I prefer to walk.'

'You do not need to bring Margaret back with you. She may stay as long as she likes. I just want to be sure of her safety.'

'I understand.'

Hannah saw him off and turned back inside. She should perhaps check on the classrooms, taking a turn herself. But if she should be called away again, that would cause yet more distress and conjecture. Something Woodward had said jogged her memory; Margaret had always liked Dr Shipley and spoken of him admiringly.

Of course — the doctor. Was it possible she had sent Mr Woodward on a wild goose chase and Margaret might have sought refuge there? But if the minister was calling for the doctor's horse on the way? No, Dr Shipley had told him just to take one; his stable lad was instructed so. Mr Woodward might not wish to waste time going to the house.

Nanny Toft was more likely — but now having this new idea, Hannah could not let it go. It would take only a few minutes for her to walk over to the doctor's house herself. It was more direct over her grounds than round by the road, and although wet and muddy in places, no problem to a pair of stout boots. She checked both classes, set more work — enough to last for a week — and turned to leave.

She hesitated for a moment. Was it a good idea to leave Lavinia alone for so long, even having Miss Hoyle and Mary Grey to help her? She remembered the chaos that had ensued last time. No, she had a better idea.

'Lavinia, could you come with me, please? I have an important errand for you. Mary is in charge here now, class. Miss Hoyle is only next door, Mary, if required.' This would be an ideal opportunity for Mary to practise

174

minding the younger girls.

What to tell Lavinia? What excuse could Hannah make for taking her with her? A chaperone was hardly necessary for an aging professional lady of twenty-seven years; marriage prospects and her reputation seemed minor matters at present.

'What is it you want me to do, Miss Hannah?' Her tone was polite enough, but Hannah thought that Lavinia resented being removed from her position of authority. She could detect a sulky twist to her lips.

'You are to accompany me, Lavinia. We are going to visit Dr Shipley. I need his assistance.'

'Dr Shipley?' Lavinia's face brightened at once.

Oh no, Hannah thought. *How could I not have noticed? Yet again. You fool, you should have kept a stricter watch; perhaps not appointed the personable doctor to attend the pupils at all.* She could have sent for an older man, to Huddersfield maybe. But Dr Shipley had been so kind in offering advantageous rates, and replacing him would have given rise to speculation in the village. As also would reversing her current decision by sending Lavinia back to the classroom. No, she was entrenched in this course now and must make the best of it.

Her purpose was wholly in seeking Margaret — but now she would be distracted by the need to watch Lavinia. She frowned as they walked up the path. Lavinia, however, was bowing her head modestly, and even Hannah could find no fault with her manner.

Dr Shipley must have seen them from his study window, for he, too, opened the door himself. 'Miss Hannah, Miss Lavinia. Is everything all right?'

'No, I am afraid it is not,' Hannah answered. 'You will have just seen Mr Woodward, of course? He was to borrow your horse.'

'Yes, he did. I am pleased about that; I count him my friend, and have put the animal completely at his disposal.'

176

'He did not say why he needed it?'

'Yes; he is helping in the search for Miss Margaret.' The doctor looked concerned. 'I was just writing out some important medical notes before coming over to offer my services. I could be of use in organising and directing the search.'

Hannah sighed. Beside her, Lavinia sighed too. A sigh of disappointment and lost opportunity, Hannah suspected. She could imagine exactly what the girl was thinking: *Why did I not consider running off, to have everyone come and look for me — and the doctor in particular?*

'Thank you. That is kindly said — but maybe at present it would be best for you to remain here in case Margaret should seek refuge with you. Or again, you may be needed if we should discover her, and . . . ' Her voice faltered. *Do not even consider that.*

'Certainly; I will wait until needed. And if you should change your mind, you have only to summon me. Would you care for some refreshment?' As she hesitated, eager to be on her way, he continued, 'There is a matter I wish to speak of. It may be of relevance.'

Hannah nodded. 'Yes, thank you. You are very kind.' She could also ask his opinion of Mr Woodward; an ideal opportunity. 'It is very generous of you to offer the minister your horse,' she began as they sat down. 'Did you know him before he came here?'

'No, but he has become a good friend very quickly. We are two professional men of an age, and both single. It was inevitable, I suppose.'

The tea cups arrived to cause a distraction. The doctor said, 'Lavinia, if we leave you to your lemonade, I am sure you will excuse us for a moment. We may retire to the window seat and admire the view of the garden. I am told it is very fine, Miss Hannah.'

It was a view Hannah had seen many times before, but she agreed politely. Her instincts were alert; there was more here than had at first seemed apparent.

She rose and Lavinia rose with them.

'I wonder,' Dr Shipley said, 'if you would consider the sampler over the fireplace for a few moments? It was done by my mother when of an age with yourself. I would value your opinion.'

Lavinia's eyebrows rose as if she knew she was being dismissed, but she contrived to look flattered and resentful at the same time.

The doctor murmured, 'You see, Miss Lavinia, there is something of a confidential nature I need to speak of. Another patient. I know you will understand. I apologise; one cannot help but appear unmannerly at times.' He nodded, and Lavinia's eyes echoed the brightness of his smile.

Hannah knew her suspicions were now confirmed. Another valuable lesson. But why this need for discretion? Surely the doctor was not about to discuss Lavinia?

'I am concerned,' Dr Shipley continued softly as they moved away. 'I wish I did not have to trouble you with this, but can see no alternative. As you will appreciate, my position is far from easy. I know I am not ill-looking, and am a member of a respected profession; and this combination can cause problems in a community consisting of so many unattached ladies.'

Hannah's eyes widened. She scanned his face, seeking a glimpse of humour, but his expression was completely serious. She said gravely, 'I see.'

'I have not seen your sister today, not since you missed her, but she *was* here yesterday. I feel I may be in part responsible for her disappearance — and yet I am certain I never encouraged her. I would never do such a thing. Being handsome is a responsibility I take seriously.'

Hannah was staring at the bland, pale eyes with fascination.

'I appreciate your sister has certain . . . problems, shall we say; and I make allowances for that, naturally. I have a professional appreciation of her difficulties. But I could not allow her to harbour the false hopes which only yesterday I discovered, to my horror, that she held dear.'

Hannah allowed herself to look politely questioning, although her heart was thudding uncomfortably. 'What false hopes do you speak of?' No, she would not assist him in this disgusting display of arrogance and self-importance.

'Why,' he said patiently, 'that Miss Margaret has developed an attachment for me. Unfortunate but inevitable, as I see now. I should perhaps have been more aloof. From our conversation yesterday, it became clear she has mistaken common courtesy for something more.'

'Poor Margaret,' Hannah said.

He sighed. 'Poor Margaret indeed. So you understand it would be unwise, if not inappropriate, for me to take an active part in the search for her. I can assure you, however, that she will not return here.'

'What did you say to her?' To think that only a few moments ago she had felt almost amused. But no longer. This surely must be the main cause of Margaret's flight. This insensitive, self-important man was completely unaware of the harm and humiliation he might have caused.

'I explained the matter to her, kindly but firmly. You need be in no fear that she was left in any doubt about the situation.'

Hannah's hands were clenched together. 'And how did she respond?'

'Well, I had to repeat myself; she seemed incapable of accepting my words at first, so it was remarkably difficult. You will appreciate this is not a situation any gentleman would wish to experience. I flatter myself I handled the matter with delicacy and tact.'

'With so much delicacy and tact that my sister has seen fit to take flight this morning,' Hannah said bitterly.

'Miss Brockley! I hope you are not blaming me in any way? I have done nothing untoward in this instance, I can assure you.'

'In this instance?' Hannah was now very angry. 'And are there other instances of this compulsive attraction to you, where you may have acted to encourage anyone?' Obviously not Margaret, she thought, and hopefully Lavinia. But what about Violet? Hannah already knew her morality had been a fragile commodity.

The doctor's face was white. His anger was now matching hers. 'I resent your implications. I think you must leave.'

She should apologise, she supposed, but the words stuck in her throat. No, she would not. Leaving — and swiftly — seemed the only choice. Already, Lavinia was taking too much interest in their muttered exchange, no longer pretending the slightest fascination with the sampler. Hannah said, quietly unforgiving, 'Would you resent them so much if any of them were suitably wealthy and worth the pursuing? But indeed, we shall leave now. Thank you for your assistance. I have learned more than I looked for.'

The doctor too was now belatedly looking over his shoulder at Lavinia. Hannah could not interpret his expression. 'Come, Lavinia,' she said.

For a moment, Hannah wondered if her pupil would rebel against the command. Fortunately, Lavinia's training overrode her disappointment. She bowed her head and turned to follow Hannah as she swept out. Although as Hannah turned briefly, entering the hall, she caught a look in Lavinia's eyes that was far from ladylike. Dr Shipley, however, did not seem to have noticed. As he had said, he was accustomed to girlish adoration. Not so accustomed to women who argued with him. Perhaps he had sensed a lack of adoration in Hannah and therefore found her disconcerting. Yet during the dinner party, she had hung on his words and returned his smiles — foolishly; she could see that now.

'I thought we would stay longer,' Lavinia said as Hannah strode down the path.

'I thought so myself.'

Lavinia's eyes narrowed. She scuffed her boots in a sulky fashion. Hannah let it pass. One should know when to make allowances. Lavinia also was about to have a severe disappointment. It seemed that three years of training and care had not had the desired results. Now must be the time to make certain matters very clear.

Hannah sighed again. It was not only Margaret and Lavinia making unwelcome discoveries this week; she was once more finding the lack in herself. She was making one mistake after another, although all based on the information she had at her disposal, which seemed to alter from minute to minute. If only she had known about Margaret's feelings for the doctor, she could have acted differently, with gentle understanding. But she did not have Margaret before her now; she had only Lavinia, and must face the present problem.

'Lavinia, you knew Violet very well.

Did she ever tell you she was attracted to the doctor?'

'Of course she was. Anyone would be.' That sly smile once more, and so reminiscent of Violet.

'And was there any sign of her attraction being returned on his part?'

Lavinia tossed her head. 'Oh, no. She was too plain, wasn't she? And as you said, she had nothing else to recommend her. Too plain and too poor.'

Hannah sighed with relief. Lavinia must be telling the truth; she would have been unable to disguise her jealousy. But Lavinia was continuing, 'You are wrong in what you said. The doctor doesn't mind girls being poor when they are pretty.'

No, no, no. This situation was more dangerous than Hannah had thought and must be nipped in the bud immediately. 'Lavinia, I believe your conduct and demeanour towards the doctor are unseemly.'

'It is all right for you — you are past marriageable age, and with your future assured; one in which you will be content. You don't seem to realise how it is for me — and was for Violet.'

'Lavinia! Hush!'

But the girl had passed the barrier of courtesy and respect towards her elders and could not stop, even if she had wanted to. 'I am alone in the world and must seek a husband while I may. What else am I to do?'

'You could have a secure future with us. I understand your situation. We will not abandon you.'

Lavinia's horrified gasp was half a sob. 'Like Miss Hoyle, and yourself and your sister? I would sooner die. That is no kind of future.'

'But it is. How wrong you are. You are an intelligent girl with a quickness of mind; why should your abilities be hidden as the chattel of some man, subjugated to his will? Marriage can be an imprisonment.'

'It is one I would gladly embrace. What is the use in sitting alone with one's cleverness in the sterile evenings, at the beck and call of other people's children? That is not for me.'

Hannah stared at her, surprised not only by Lavinia's response but the passion that had arisen within herself. She shook her head. 'You are mistaken.'

Lavinia turned and set off blindly to where the path across the lower field sloped upwards. Hannah called, 'Where are you going?'

Lavinia turned. 'I am imprisoned, whatever happens. I have to ask someone's permission before I eat or sleep or even breathe, or walk to the village to purchase sewing thread.'

'We all must,' Hannah said.

'Not you.'

'I am not as free as you think. The responsibility for the well-being of all of you rests on my shoulders.' Hannah bit her lip. 'I have duties and responsibilities in my life, as do all women, married or not. I have only sought to equip you for the lives you must lead. But whether you feel you need a husband or not, there are right

188

and wrong ways of going about this.'

As she turned, Lavinia said something. Hannah said coldly, 'I beg your pardon?' But she already knew that Lavinia had muttered, 'And how would *you* know?' The girl's rudeness was insufferable and should be dealt with by a suitable punishment, but Hannah knew she was right. How could *she* talk about the ways to find a husband? Hannah felt weary of it all and she could not help but sympathise with Lavinia. Her heart ached at the thought of such an arid and dutiful future, particularly if one had no calling or aptitude for teaching.

If the school had been larger, perhaps Lavinia would have found more friends of her own age; could have been invited to their homes in the holidays, and introduced to brothers and cousins who might have been attracted to that perfect face and inspired to offer marriage. But those same brothers and relatives would also have careful parents who would be unlikely to approve of their sons seeking marriage with a penniless girl, however beautiful.

And what of her own future? *If the school fails and Margaret and I sell the house and live somewhere smaller, the sale will provide an income we may survive upon, but little else. It would be an empty future.* She shivered. The coming years seemed every bit as bleak as those confronting Lavinia.

And what of Margaret? She was a beloved weight around her neck. And however much she strove to do her best for her sister, Margaret would always find her wanting and tell her so. Worse than that, she always thought Hannah was deliberately putting her own interests first, to Margaret's detriment.

Hannah sighed. Where had this resentment begun? Far back in their childhood, when Hannah was indisputably their father's favourite. Foolishly, she had taken too much pride in his esteem; even boasted of it if she and Margaret argued. She winced. Not an aspect of herself she cared to remember. Poor Father. Surely he could never have realised the harm he was doing. Such a complex, brilliant man, wanting to achieve the best for his family. What would he think if he could see his daughters now? No safe marriage for Hannah with Sir George to bring Margaret safety and security also. She had hoped their father would have been proud of the way she had overcome the obstacles in her path. She now suspected he would have found her wanting.

Lavinia was out of sight. Hannah found herself looking across the grounds in the direction Mr Woodward would have taken on the doctor's horse to find Nanny Toft. Margaret must surely be there, but once Hannah knew for certain, she would feel more settled. She could then return to the other problems of Violet's death and the inquest Sir George must arrange.

Wait. As the hall chimneys appeared over to her left, she stopped. By far the best thing for Margaret was to stay with Nanny Toft, who would mother her and care for her and bring her back to a state of sense and composure. But what about the inquest? Would Sir George seek to call her as a witness? No, he must not. That would undo all the good of her stay with their old nurse. Surely he would not be so heartless, knowing the ordeal it would be for her?

She must face facts. Of course he would. Remembering how Margaret had spoken out to him, with no sign of hesitation or fear, and the nature of what she had said, he would be bound to insist on her presence.

It must not happen. As always, it was Hannah's duty to protect Margaret. If Sir George intended to bring the truth of Violet's behaviour and even her condition into the public eye, there were others who could testify to that. She would tell him so.

She glanced ahead. Lavinia must be almost back by now; Hannah would never catch her up. She made her decision. This would take very little time and do so much good. Already she was turning aside and hurrying off in the direction of the hall.

9

Hannah adjusted her bonnet and straightened her dress before ringing the bell. Suddenly this arrival did not seem suitably formal. Strange, when she and Margaret had been such frequent visitors as children without a second thought. And after their father's death, Sir George had been such a source of help and comfort — at first. It was since his marriage that she had felt much less welcome. Lady Foxcroft was always aware of the formalities.

Now the butler was staring down at her; she was conscious of how she must appear to him. 'I wish to see Sir George, please.'

'I am sorry, madam, but Sir George is not at home.'

She stared at him coldly, filled with frustration. One never knew whether the words could be taken for truth or whether Sir George did not wish to see her, although she could not think why he might not. She said meaningfully, 'Ah,' wanting to add that she would wait. But of course that was hardly practical; she could not afford the time.

'It is all right, Meadows. I shall receive Miss Hannah.' Lady Foxcroft's voice came from the stairs. She sailed down gracefully, arms outstretched in greeting as if her entrance had been deliberate. 'How delightful to see you. An all too infrequent occurrence. Come into the drawing room.' She seated herself, gesturing to the chair Hannah might occupy. 'And of course, you must not stand on ceremony with us. You were absolutely right to dismiss your chaperone.'

'My . . . ? Oh, you mean Lavinia. But that must have been a quarter of an hour ago.' The chair Lady Foxcroft had indicated was uncomfortable, putting her at a disadvantage already.

'Yes, you have caught me out. In my weakened state of health, my major occupation and delight is to observe the comings and goings from the windows of my dressing room. I have made it quite the little sanctuary. Sir George teases me, you know. He tells me that nothing escapes me.' There was a look in her eye as if to give the words a significance Hannah could not make out. Something to think about later. Hannah had the uneasy feeling this was what Lady Foxcroft had intended.

Hannah tried to regain her composure. 'Miss Lavinia had to fulfil an errand.'

'Of course.' Lady Foxcroft's smile spoke of complicity.

Was she underestimating Lady Foxcroft? Hannah had no idea of where this might be leading. 'It was unavoidable.'

'Now, I do not compliment myself that your visit was purely social. How may I help you?'

Hannah hesitated. 'I was merely wishing to consult with Sir George about the inquest. And really, since he is not here, I feel I should trouble you no longer.'

Lady Foxcroft pouted a little. 'You cannot leave so soon. If you do not stay, I declare I shall feel quite put out. You will have me thinking — as does the whole of this locality — that you are only interested in seeing my husband rather than myself. What kind of unwelcoming message does that convey to a new bride?'

Hannah tried to smile. 'Indeed not. And you are hardly a new bride now; you have been married for almost five years.'

'A length of time that is apparently seared into your heart. I see you do not deny your interest in my husband?'

Lady Foxcroft's words were outrageous, but Hannah tried to remain calm. 'I wished to speak to him on a professional matter as local magistrate. You can surely understand that — and that I have no other motive.'

But the words were tumbling from Lady Foxcroft almost before Hannah could finish speaking in her own defence. 'No, you cannot deny it. This death has provided a fortunate excuse for you to be hanging about around him, summoning him to the school at all hours and upon the smallest pretexts. And now you seek to come and invade my privacy and solitude; which, I may tell you, I hold most dear.'

Hannah stared at her, taken aback by the change in mood. 'I had to report the death to Sir George, and it was he who felt bound to investigate the circumstances thoroughly. That was nothing to do with me.'

'So you say. Since you have had to languish in your reluctant spinsterhood for those five years and more, it is a pity you did not hit upon such a ploy earlier, finding excuses to seek his assistance.'

'I beg your pardon? I assure you, Lady Foxcroft, nothing can be further from the truth.'

'You cannot deny you expected to marry my husband. No, of course you cannot. That is common knowledge here.'

Hannah rose, maintaining a dignified stance. 'Lady Foxcroft, you are over-wrought. I am sorry to have troubled you. I had no idea you had such an intensity of feeling about this — and completely erroneous, I assure you. If I had any expectation of Sir George, I relinquished all such when he chose you.'

Lady Foxcroft put a hand to her brow, breathing heavily. 'I wish I could believe that. You do not know how I suffer, contemplating the truth of these unfortunate circumstances.'

'There is no need for suffering,' Hannah said firmly. 'On either side. I have no regrets; I am happy running my school. I know a union between us was something my father would have wished, but I could not have brought Sir George a suitable marriage portion, so it would not have done. I speak frankly only because you have done so. I do not intend to broach this subject again. Indeed, if you feel like this, I do not intend to come here again. You have no grounds for these accusations, I can assure you; but if my presence upsets you, you shall not be troubled with me. I shall only communicate with Sir George when strictly necessary, and then through a third party, such as the Reverend Woodward or Dr Shipley. I will wish you a good day. Do not trouble to ring. I will let myself out.'

There was no need for her to access the front door alone, of course, as there were at least two servants hovering in the hall. No doubt Lady Foxcroft's hysterical voice had penetrated the drawing-room door while Hannah's more measured tones had not, but it was too late to worry about that now. There would inevitably be a new tale to be spread around the village, along with the erroneous information with which Lady Foxcroft had been fuelling her jealousy. Her servants would have set their minds upon a good story, and there would be no stopping them.

Hannah could only hope those who were loyal to her, such as Millie and Tom and Mrs Copley, would speak against any lies they heard. She said, 'Thank you, Meadows. I am leaving now.'

He bowed his head, barely concealing a knowing smile. As he turned to the door, however, the bell jangled again, followed by a furious knocking. 'Have I to ring my own bell now? Have I not trained you to be alert to my approach?'

Meadows hastily opened the door as Sir George was upon them. 'I am sorry, Sir George. I did not hear your horse.'

'I was on foot, man.'

Hannah stared at him. His face was pale, and sweat beaded his brow as he berated them. 'Why are you all standing about here? Can a man not enter his own home without fuss? Go away.' He saw Hannah and stopped abruptly. 'Ah, Miss Hannah. My apologies.'

Hannah bowed her head in acknowledgement. 'I was just leaving.' But without the information she sought, which was still important. If she left and asked Mr Woodward to return on her behalf, that would be further delay and of little use to Margaret. Her duty to her sister came first. 'Yes, I was just leaving — but perhaps you could answer my query quite quickly? I merely wish to know when the inquest is to be held.'

'The inquest.'

'Yes, for Violet. For you see, I am concerned about my sister.' She explained briefly.

As she spoke, Sir George became visibly calmer. 'Of course, of course. I am sorry to hear of her absence, but I understand. If she has found a safe haven, I am sure we may proceed without her. By all means.'

Hannah had not expected such an easy victory. 'That is most welcome. You are too good, Sir George,' she said warmly. She stopped, conscious that ardent gratitude could easily be misinterpreted by his wife, who was now standing in the doorway to the drawing room.

She resisted the urge to turn and gauge Lady Foxcroft's awareness. That would only make things worse. In spite of herself, however, her eyes were sliding and her head tilting and to her surprise, Lady Foxcroft seemed to be smiling. Hannah said, 'Do we know the day the inquest might be held?'

'Certainly. I am arranging it at the White Hart within the next few days. Tuesday, maybe.'

'So soon? That is good news. You must be convinced there is nothing more to be discovered?'

'Exactly so. As you are aware, my investigations have been most thorough. Thus, the inquest itself may be necessarily brief.'

Hannah smiled. 'It is a great relief to me to hear you say so. I only wish to have it over and done with so I know what I am to do next. As you are aware, the verdict will necessarily affect the school.' The wave of relief had caused her to say more than she intended.

Sir George cut her off with a barking laugh. 'Say no more of your situation, I beg you — else you may be found guilty of importuning a magistrate.'

Hannah flushed. 'Oh, I am sorry; I did not think. I was not aware of such legislation.'

'Neither am I, I believe. Merely my little joke. No more than that. Well, Hannah, we need trouble you no further. The weather looks to be on the turn and the park is muddy enough already. I should avoid the lower path by the stream if I were you. Not a route suitable for a lady's feet.'

'Thank you for your advice.' She would not argue when he was in such a favourable mood, and even Lady Foxcroft was nodding graciously, but she had no intention of taking it. The path by the stream was more direct; and from the further part of it, she would be able to intercept Mr Woodward if he should be on his way back.

Sir George said, 'In fact, wait a few

moments and one of my servants can escort you.'

She was surprised. As if she would need an escort to cross her own land, or Sir George's. 'That is most kind; but as you said, there are some threatening clouds about now. I would rather not wait; and I do agree, the upper path is much the drier.'

She strode out stoutly, wanting only to get back. The encounters had been strange in many ways, particularly with Lady Foxcroft, but at least Hannah now had the information she required and could reassure Margaret as soon as possible. Hannah smiled — always supposing Margaret would not be in one of her contrary moods and decide she *would* like to be a witness. At last, however, she was feeling she could see the way out of this nightmare that had begun — goodness, was it only two days ago? It seemed so much longer. A lifetime. Forever. *Now you are being overdramatic*, she told herself.

She paused for a last sighting of the

road where Mr Woodward would come, before dropping down to the stream. She hurried down the slope, knowing that as the bank rose on the other side beyond the stepping stones, her view would be restored. And it was hardly muddy at all. Sir George must have a strange view of a lady's capabilities; but now he would be governed by his wife, no doubt, and *her* opinions.

Smiling, Hannah strode out a little too confidently. Her boot slid on a loose pebble where a scattering of stones and earth lay across the path as if some animal had disturbed the bank. One minute she was upright, arms flailing, and the next she was hitting the ground. She lay there, regaining her breath. She thought, *you are proved right, Sir George. Fortunate that there is no one to see me.* What a foolish picture she must present, with being so careless. Her own fault.

She began to realise her right hand was not resting on grass and earth as she might expect. She could feel the softness of fabric, the smoothness of leather. She opened her eyes and fought the scream. She had dislodged newly dug earth and her hand was resting on a small shoe-clad foot.

Oh, no. No, no, no. She wanted to run without looking, never finding out what lay there. But of course she could not.

She pulled at the bushes and scrub still covering the form, recognising the cloak and the dress. There was no doubt at all. She had only seen the girl less than an hour ago. *Lavinia. An accident*, she thought wildly. Earth and bushes dislodged, the ground still icy where it was not muddy; had the bank given way as Lavinia had trod unwarily? And perhaps she was not too late.

'Lavinia,' she called, putting her cheek to the contorted mouth. Foolish again. The girl's eyes were wide open. There could be no mistake. She was dead.

10

Against all logic, however, Hannah's hands and voice were refusing to believe it. She continued shaking the girl's shoulders, calling her name. But she stopped as abruptly as she had started. If this should not be an accident, she could be destroying valuable evidence as to what had happened. She must inform Sir George at once. At least this time he was near at hand.

She struggled to her feet and climbed back the way she had come. If he sent out the hue and cry straightaway, they might even discover the murderer. As so might she. She looked round nervously, but the landscape was as empty as it had been when she arrived. Obviously the perpetrator would not wait to be discovered. There was only the hall, brooding over the scene as before.

Heedless of dignity or comfort, she ran back along the path, panic rising in her breast, her heart beating too fast. But she needed to act, to move quickly, anything to put as much distance as possible between herself and the poor bedraggled thing that had been Lavinia — pretty, petulant, determined, and deceptively sweet when it pleased her, and now no more.

No. She made herself stop and take a breath. Panic would help no one, least of all Lavinia, who was beyond all help. Panic only bred further panic. Hannah began to walk briskly but firmly, taking long strides. The hall seemed much further than when she had come. Her only refuge. Once there, she would be safe. Lavinia had still been warm. That meant her killer could still be near at hand. *Be calm.* Why should he wait here to reveal himself? He had obviously striven to hide the body, perhaps hoping it would not be discovered for weeks.

At last, Hannah made herself close

the small gate into Sir George's inner garden with care. It was a strange feeling, when she had gone through this gate and taken the same path little more than an hour ago. Now everything was irretrievably different. Nothing could ever be the same again.

She rang the bell, and Meadows opened the door. Once again, Lady Foxcroft was descending the stairs. 'It is all right, Meadows. You return so soon, Miss Hannah?'

'Yes. There has been . . . the most terrible accident. I must speak to Sir George with the utmost urgency.' Lady Foxcroft's eyebrows rose. Hannah added belatedly, 'If you please.'

'Sir George is feeling a little indisposed at present. May I help?'

'Indisposed? But I saw him here not half an hour ago. He is needed in his official capacity. It is a matter of extreme urgency.'

Lady Foxcroft nodded kindly. 'I see you have been quite affected by it, whatever it is. Pray be calm, Miss

Hannah. Come and sit down.'

Hannah could hardly believe what she was hearing. 'Whatever your feelings for me are, Lady Foxcroft, I do pray that you lay them aside. This is important. A young woman — Lavinia, one of our pupils — lies dead by the stream.'

'Another pupil? Dear me. And Sir George recommended that you take the higher route away from the stream. I recall that particularly.'

'And if I had, I would not have found her. Who knows how long she would have lain there? It is too late to help her now, but it is unseemly for her body to be lying out at the mercy of the elements any longer than need be.' She could have screamed in frustration. 'I should not need to explain this. I know it must be upsetting for you, occurring almost on your doorstep, but I find your response inappropriate.'

'And I find your words ill-mannered in the extreme.'

Hannah stood up, recognising Sir

211

George's footsteps with relief. 'Sir George, at last! Please come with me at once. Lavinia is dead by the stream.' She lowered her voice. 'I do not wish to cause alarm, but I think there may be similarities to the way Violet died.'

'This is terrible.' The words were appropriate, but Sir George seemed distant, almost as if he were not in the least surprised. But then Lady Foxcroft had already stated he was feeling unwell — though he looked healthy enough otherwise. He coughed. 'But have no fear; you have obviously performed your duty in reporting the event to me. I shall see to it. Would you like the body to be brought back here? To take her to the school would be distressing for the other young ladies, when they have been distressed enough.'

'That is very kind.' Hannah hesitated. 'And yet I would not wish to try to avoid my responsibilities to Lavinia.' A sob rose in her throat, and subduing it almost caused her to choke. But she must not show any further weakness.

'I doubt anyone will think that,' Lady Foxcroft said. 'I am sure you have always performed them only too well.'

Hannah frowned. What could she mean? She decided to ignore the remark as another instance of Lady Foxcroft's odd behaviour.

'And of course,' Sir George said, 'I will not need to interview anyone else at the school this time. Only yourself.'

'Myself?'

'You would have been the last person to see Miss Lavinia alive. That is what you said, as I understand it.'

'Did I say that?' It was true, of course — but when had she said so? She was finding concentration difficult, though it was not surprising after the shock she had experienced.

'Miss Hannah, you are distraught and quite distracted,' Lady Foxcroft said kindly. 'Please come in and sit down.'

'No, thank you. I must get back. Unless . . . surely you do not wish to interview me straightaway?'

'Indeed not,' said Sir George. 'I am not such a monster. Go back and endeavour to collect yourself. One of our maids will accompany you. After such a dreadful experience, you must not be alone.'

'No, I would not impose. But as I said, I do believe Lavinia also may have been murdered, and the killer may still be out there.'

'Your safety will be uppermost in all our minds,' Lady Foxcroft said, as if to a nervous child. 'An under-footman will go with you as well. Two men, even.'

'No, I was not thinking of myself. But it is only common sense, surely. I mean, should you not . . . would not a search of the area be advisable?'

Sir George nodded. 'Yes, indeed. Be assured, we shall do everything necessary.'

'Come, Miss Hannah,' Lady Foxcroft said. 'I really do not think you are in any danger at all. And you must know that as well as I.'

Hannah shook her head, trying to

clear it. She had no time for Lady Foxcroft's enigmatic remarks. She had always been a little distant, even wary, with Hannah, but today Hannah felt she was responding with a complete lack of sense. Perhaps she meant that Hannah was in no danger because Lavinia and Violet had been young and pretty? A remark completely lacking in taste, in the circumstances. No, she must feel sorry for Lady Foxcroft's insecurity; based, Hannah presumed, on unfounded jealousy. She must be kind and not condemn her.

Sir George said almost sharply to his wife, 'Take Miss Hannah into the withdrawing room for a few moments while I give my instructions.'

'Yes, my dear. Would you care for refreshment while you wait for one of the men?' The offer was within a hair's breadth of being ungracious.

Hannah had already refused all this, hadn't she? She was no longer sure. 'No, thank you.' But the refreshment was pressed upon her. In spite of herself, she was finding the glass of cordial most welcome. Her skin felt clammy. Sitting down had not been a good idea. She would have been better keeping on the move. She took a couple of sips and set the glass down.

Sir George was back. 'All agreed. A party to bring the body here — when I have inspected it *in situ*, of course, and the surrounding site. A party to search the grounds. And your escorts are gathered in the hall. This is all as you wished, is it not?'

Hannah was no longer at all sure what she had wanted, but one course of action seemed as good as another. There was an uneasy feeling that she had forgotten something, the memory quashed by the horrific events of the morning. Why had she come here? What had been her original purpose?

She allowed Lady Foxcroft to help her to her feet. There were murmured remarks around her. 'If you are sure you would not rather remain here and rest?'

'If you are sure this is what you wish?'

'No, she is right. She will be better at home.'

They were becoming irritable. Hannah wished Sir George and Lady Foxcroft would keep their arguments for a more appropriate time and place.

She was being escorted to the door for the second time that day. The two manservants seemed just as determined as their masters to ensure that she set off, and also presumably that she arrived at her destination. She resented the proprietary grip upon her arms but could not summon up the will to do anything about it. Of course she had experienced a terrible shock. No wonder she could hardly think straight.

They paused at the gate; it was not so easy for the three of them together to edge through, as there was hardly room on the path — not as easy as she had arrived in her flight to seek refuge. And had she found it? She did not know.

She raised her head. What was that

217

sound? The clouds in her head fell away and she remembered her original purpose. She had been looking for Margaret. What had ailed her that she had forgotten so soon? Except that she must still be in the grip of some kind of delirium, because she was almost convinced she could hear her sister's voice.

'Hannah! Please don't go.'

The gate was open. The men were taking her arms firmly once more and moving forward. 'This way, Miss Brockley.'

Hannah said, 'No, wait.' The voice was not the result of some hysterical delusion within her head. She looked upwards, past the first floor where Lady Foxcroft had told her she spent her days, and above, to the smaller rooms on the top floor, where the servants might sleep. One of the small windows was open to the chill of the icy air as a hand waved through it, and the voice came again: 'Hannah, help me.'

She reacted instinctively and perhaps

218

unwisely. 'That is Margaret!' she exclaimed. With a swift movement that surprised the two men, she twisted herself free and was back down the path and into the house. 'Margaret is here. I demand to see her.'

'Margaret? What is this?' Sir George said. 'What do you mean?'

'I came seeking her. She had run away. Why did no one tell me she was here?'

'You never asked me. You merely wanted to know about the inquest.'

'I am certain I asked your wife.'

'Well, I am not answerable for whatever she may have said. Come in, my dear. We must address the situation anew.'

'I wish to see my sister immediately.'

'That is very understandable. Of course you do. Come with me.' Sir George put a hand upon her arm, leading her towards the stairs and dismissing the two servants with a brusque nod.

Hannah followed. 'And why is she

confined? Why is she calling for help?' For the first time, she realised how her speech and actions might have been unwise. However distressing for Margaret, the wiser course would have been to leave quietly and return with witnesses to whatever was said. Now she was here alone; there was no longer any sign even of the servants. And they would hardly act in her favour, but would support their employer.

Sir George shrugged. 'Why does your sister choose to do anything? Who knows?'

Hannah bit her lip, wanting to tell him he must not underestimate Margaret; sometimes she chose a course of action or words merely for dramatic effect. Hannah was more experienced than anyone else at perceiving the difference.

They had reached the topmost corridor. 'Here,' Sir George said, lowering his voice so that Hannah found herself instinctively lowering hers.

She said, 'But is she all right? She seemed distressed when I heard her.'

He opened a door, ushering her in. The room was empty. 'Margaret?' Hannah called suddenly; and the answering cry, full of relief, was from another room further along. Hannah said angrily, 'Take me to her. At once, if you please.'

With a harsh hand at one elbow and the other between her shoulder blades, Hannah was swiftly propelled into the room. Sir George's voice was like ice. 'I did not wish to do this, but you leave me no alternative. This is for your sister's good as well as yours. As magistrate, I must confine you here. Your sister has made very serious accusations against you. She must be protected from the very person who had the closest duty to protect *her*.'

'What are you talking about?'

'I am afraid that a denial is not sufficient. I must confine you here until my investigations can be renewed and completed. And of course you may wish to hasten this very sad affair by admitting the whole, straightaway. We shall take care of Margaret, you may be assured of that.'

Hannah shook her head. She could make no sense of any of this. 'I don't understand.'

'My dear, it grieves me sincerely, but I have to tell you I know everything. You have committed murder, not once but again this very morning. We have your sister's account and know the deplorable truth.'

'No. How can you think that?'

'I can tell you no more. But I will say that we have your sister's testimony. And I have made my own observations also. There is little doubt left in me. Having known you both for so long, I am deeply saddened. Your father's memory is ever at the forefront of my mind, and what he would have thought.' He shook his head sadly. 'But now I will leave you here to reflect upon the substance of your confession when I return later.'

'No, wait. You must listen to me.' But she was faced only with the solid white panels of the closed door. She raised her hands, thinking to bang on them and demand her release. But no — she would not give Lady Foxcroft such an opportunity to gloat. It was bad enough that she had foolishly allowed herself to be put in this position. Everything had happened so quickly.

Was this even within the law? Her knowledge of legal matters was sparse. Besides, here, Sir George *was* the law. He must surely know what he was doing. She must trust in him to examine the evidence and arrive at a correct conclusion.

She could only hope he would not be influenced by Lady Foxcroft's jealousy, if he had not been so affected already. Perhaps it was Lady Foxcroft she must thank for putting her in this situation. Yes, that made sense. Lady Foxcroft was capitalising on poor Margaret's unfortunate ramblings, not because she believed them but because they suited her purpose. That purpose being to make trouble for the rival she still feared.

If only Hannah had realised the depth of Lady Foxcroft's dislike earlier. But nothing would be served by thinking what might or could have been done. She must consider what action she could take now. The first opportunity would be when Sir George returned to hear her supposed confession. She must use that time to convince him of her innocence. At least she had truth on her side; and surely the truth, told simply and concisely, must always triumph?

Mr Woodward, she thought. He would believe her. She allowed herself a brief smile, thinking of him. If only she had curbed her impatience and arranged for the minister to accompany her here. She would have welcomed his opinion on the events of this morning. He could have spoken for her, because he would believe in her. Although was that not a little unfair, when she had not always believed in him?

She could see now how unlikely it was that there should be any foundation in her earlier suspicions about Mr Woodward. Not if the same killer had murdered both girls, as seemed likely. She had watched for his return on the only route he might take and without any sight of him. Would he have taken a different route? The only alternatives would have been much further, and he could hardly have got here in the time, even if he had turned straight round at Nanny Toft's sister's house and come back. Whoever Lavinia's killer was, the murderer could not have known he would come across her by the stream, and at that particular time.

Thank goodness she was now convinced of Mr Woodward's innocence. The strength of her relief took her by surprise. She had not wanted it to be him — or anyone she knew; but least of all him.

But why was Margaret here? If only she could communicate with her sister in some way. But as soon as Sir George had locked the door, Hannah could no longer hear her cries. Besides, anything shouted at full voice would be audible to their captors and therefore useless.

She must think of all the alternatives and decide what would be practicable. No doubt she had plenty of time. It did not seem that Sir George was in any hurry for this confession. They would have to feed her, surely? If Sir George had designated these rooms as a temporary prison, he must provide food and drink. How would this be managed? Were there any servants who might be sympathetic? Maybe her knowledge of village connections and family ties would work in her favour. Sir George had always tended to keep aloof from the local area. And his longstanding servants would remember her father as a frequent visitor — and his daughters, too, as children. Were any of those older ones still here?

If she had the good fortune to recognise anyone who would be sympathetic to her, what would be the best way forward? Perhaps she could send a message to Mr Woodward? Without criticising Sir George in any way, of course, because a note might well fall into the wrong hands. Just asking him to come here and speak for her, perhaps. It might be worth a try — if she had anything to write with, or on. Of course she did not. It would have to be a verbal message, after all.

She looked around the room, but there was nothing to help her; just a chair and a basic truckle bed. It was a room obviously intended for servants originally, but it now would function equally well as a prison. She shuddered. Surely they would not attempt to keep her here long?

★　★　★

Hours passed. Hannah would not have thought herself capable of sleeping here in these circumstances; but as the room darkened and she found herself swaying in the chair, she lay down on the bed. Her last bitter thoughts were that at least they could have left her a candle, and how she hoped that Margaret was being treated in a more kindly fashion.

She woke to hear the door being unlocked. She tried to recover her thoughts. What had she hoped to achieve with one of the servants? A kindly face she might recognise? The idea was quashed at once, however. Of course Lady Foxcroft had made her own replacements and additions to her staff. The servant opening the door was one of these, accompanied by the grim-faced manservant who had been given the duty of escorting her home. And surprisingly, in spite of the early hour, here also was Lady Foxcroft herself. Had she come as an extra precaution, or to gloat yet again? Hannah could not decide, but was soon to find out.

Lady Foxcroft was nodding. 'Yes, this seems suitable. I wished to come and inspect your quarters for myself. But I have to say, I was shocked and horrified to discover that keeping you here has been necessary.'

'It is not, I can assure you. If Sir George wants me to make some kind of statement, I do not need to be locked up in order to do so. Surely you cannot approve of this?'

'Ah, but it will concentrate the mind wonderfully, I am sure.'

'How long must I stay here? I did not expect to stay all night. I can make my statement as soon as he wishes.'

'Some while yet, I fear. Sir George has been dealing with the practicalities of retrieving the girl's body. He has been up half the night dealing with the situation you have caused.'

'And what about Margaret? Why is she also locked in? According to Sir George, she is the victim in this situation.'

'This is for Margaret's own protection. We are determined no harm will come to her while she is under our roof. Now, I must leave you. I should not be discussing such details.'

Hannah resisted the strong urge to call out to Lady Foxcroft to wait; her gaoler would enjoy her pleading immensely. She looked down at the food that had been set down on the floor: a plate of dry bread, a small piece of cheese and a flask of water. It would be laughable if the situation had not been so serious. Lady Foxcroft had swept in to bring her fare fit for a prisoner. Hannah wondered whether Sir George even knew anything of her visit. And surely yesterday he would have arranged to recover Lavinia's body at once?

She placed her ear to the door, and yes, they were also taking food to Margaret. They would have to; presumably she had already been here for several hours when Hannah discovered her. She turned to look at the rest of the room. Margaret had attracted her attention by opening the window. There was one here also, set at head height; and by grasping the sill, she could just see out. She, too, could try attracting attention, as Margaret had done.

Most of the tradesmen and visitors would use the drive with their carts and carriages, however. Only those on foot used this way — through the small garden, the paddock, and then the school grounds. Besides, that would not be successful twice. No doubt there was a man positioned below her to guard against it. They might even board the window up if she did, depriving her of light. Lady Foxcroft would be capable of that.

No, she would be better doing as Sir George and Lady Foxcroft had advised. She must go over all the recent events that seemed to condemn her so she could recall everything clearly and in a way that would only emphasise her innocence.

'Hannah!'

She turned, startled. How could that be Margaret's voice when the door was still tightly closed? She moved over to the door, cupping a hand to one ear, but now the voice was even fainter.

Cautiously, not wanting to alert anyone else in the house, she said, 'Margaret?'

'Over here.'

Hannah turned, confused. It was as if the voice came from behind her — but how, when the room was empty? She felt disorientated, unable to accept the evidence of her own senses.

'Hurry, Hannah. You have to open it. I can't; not from this side.'

'Where are you?'

'Inside the wall. Behind the panelling. Surely you remember?'

'Oh! No, I don't remember that.' She only recalled how they had played in and around the hall. 'You knew all the hiding places. I could never find you.'

'I told you, I can't open it from the inside. Have you forgotten everything that matters?' Margaret's voice was impatient.

'Yes. No. It was so long ago. And you played by yourself so often.' Hannah was running her hands over the panelling as she spoke. 'Being older, I was spending my time downstairs with

Sir George's sisters.'

'With his sisters? I don't think so. *You* were wasting your time trying to entrap a husband who never did come up to scratch.'

Annoyed, Hannah pressed harder; the panels creaked and swung and Margaret almost fell into the room. Margaret said, 'And never would have done, because we had no money, or not enough.'

Hannah hugged her, not even troubling to rebuke her for the ill-timed remarks. Margaret broke away first. 'We have no time for discussing your romantic and matrimonial failings. I called as loudly as I dared all night. I thought you would never wake. We are in grave danger.'

11

There was no point in protesting that Margaret had started that topic. Hannah found herself smiling, partly with relief and partly at the unusual gravity in Margaret's volatile face. She stopped quickly, aware that Margaret would take the smile the wrong way.

As she did. 'Why must you always laugh at me? And more than any, now is not the time for that, when our lives may depend on what we do.'

Must everything become a melodrama? Hannah held her tongue, saying only, 'I know. I don't understand why we have been imprisoned, but we must trust Sir George and English justice to sort everything out.'

Margaret snorted her disbelief. 'There, I knew it. You still have a fondness for him, whatever he does. If you trust Sir George, you will end up dead, like poor

Lavinia. And me with you, which is even more to the purpose from my point of view.'

'Surely not. Why are you saying this? You cannot just come out with serious accusations like this.'

'You are so annoying, Hannah. Sometimes I could scream at you. Look — this passage behind the panelling goes the whole length of this top floor. Although as you saw, once in, you can't get out without outside help.'

'Yes. These were priest holes, were they not? And you would not want your forbidden priests emerging at inopportune moments.'

Margaret frowned. 'I don't know about them. Whoever they were, they are not here now, so why do you mention them? But there is another advantage of the passageway. There are places where you can hear what people are saying on the floor below. And I have heard Sir George and Lady Foxcroft talking. That's how I know.'

'Know what?'

'That they mean to kill us.' Margaret threw her hands up above her head. 'There, I knew you wouldn't believe me.'

'I know how you sometimes exaggerate,' Hannah said gently. 'You must surely have gained the wrong impression. He cannot actually have used those words.'

'Dispose of us, he said. What else could he mean by that? I heard him, as clear as day. Well, you sit here and await your fate then, if all you can do is laugh and shake your head, and see if I care. But I am not sitting here with you.'

'I shall take this seriously, I promise. After all, we have been locked in and kept apart.'

Margaret tugged at her arm. 'Come with me now and listen.'

'Margaret, there is no guarantee they will be discussing us now at this very moment, or even be within the right rooms. They are probably downstairs. And I *do* believe you heard their talk. Why do we not sit here calmly while you tell me exactly what you heard?'

'You always put obstacles in the way, Madam Calm. If you were not so eager to do so, I could have stayed at home from the first. But no one listens to me.'

'*I* wish to listen to you.' Hannah thought quickly. In arguing, she was not helping at all. 'All right, I will come with you first, and you may show me where the passages go and where you can hear the voices — and then we will return here and decide what to do next.'

Margaret brightened. 'Come, then.' And with a twist of her body and a skilful manipulation of her skirts, she was through the opening and gone.

'Wait — I don't know if I can get in there. However did you manage that?' It looked so dark and narrow. Hannah suppressed a shudder, gritted her teeth and slid in. She was not sure what she had been expecting, but nothing as finished and sophisticated as this. The passages must have been constructed at the same time as the house, so well made were they, and concealed cleverly in the thickness of the wall. There were even small slits to act as windows, just wide enough to give a modicum of light without being visible from the outside. It was a practical touch, as if those concealed should be blundering about in the dark and might give themselves away.

Hannah's fascination overcame her fear of the confined space. She caught up to where Margaret was waiting for her. 'See, this is my room. It's just like yours, but they have brought me books and a washstand because they kept saying I was their guest. They said they locked the door to keep my presence secret apart from the most trusted servants. And to keep me safe.' She nodded. 'But then I began to think more clearly about it, and I decided I had been too hasty and wanted to go home, but they would not let me. Lady Foxcroft said they knew best and I must abide by their superior sense. I screamed and said they were keeping me prisoner against my will, but they brought that large one and he stood by me to threaten me until I was quiet. He had a big staff in his hands. So I pretended to do as they said, and was quiet until I saw Lavinia across the paddock by the stream.'

'You saw Lavinia? Did you see anyone else with her?' Hannah held her breath.

'No. Those trees beyond the paddock hide that part of the view. But I saw you coming along the path from the doctor's house and making your way here. I tried to call out then, but I struggled to open the window, and then you were inside and it was too late.'

'That was a brave thing to do.'

'Yes. I didn't know what they would do if they heard me. And I am glad I did, since now I have told you of our danger, you will know what to do.' She paused. 'Except that now you are in danger, too.'

Such trust. Hannah did not know whether to laugh or cry. She hoped

Margaret's confidence in her was not misplaced. She must demonstrate it was not. She straightened her shoulders. 'Never mind about me. You did completely the right thing.'

Margaret was looking at her expectantly. 'What shall we do now?'

'Have you explored the full extent of the passage? Is there no other way out except into these other rooms?'

'There is a stairway at the end, where the wall turns the corner.'

'Good. Let me see.' It was more than she had hoped, presumably a spiral stair in the thickness of the wall. If it led upwards, it might take them out to the roof, as so often happened in churches and old castles. If they could not climb down somehow from there, they could at least attract attention.

She followed Margaret to the corner and her hopes were at once quashed. The spiral staircase went only downwards. No doubt in the old times it was thought that an exit at roof level would be too easily discovered. She tried to hide her disappointment. 'Where does it go?'

'Just down.' Margaret ran down the narrow steps nimbly until Hannah was beginning to feel dizzy. There must surely be a way out. The secret priests would not want to be caught like rats in a trap. Except that she seemed to remember hearing or reading about unfortunate clerics who *had* met that fate.

Margaret stopped abruptly so that Hannah was swaying on her stair. 'This is all of it.' Before them was a wall of new, clean stone.

'Yes,' Hannah said, as her hopes were again destroyed. 'I had forgotten the new ballroom and Lady Foxcroft's improvements.' Here, the original layout of the house had been altered.

'It is said to be very fine,' Margaret said wistfully.

'No doubt. Strange there was no talk of secret passages discovered when the work was being done. Ah, Lady Foxcroft would not trust local workmen, I remember now. She brought builders up from London. They had their own camp on the paddock and were not allowed to mix with the villagers, even had they wanted to.'

So the stairs could not be of use. What else? As they retraced their steps, Hannah took care to examine the walls more carefully. As well as the slits admitting the light, there were slits to the inner rooms. They were guest bedrooms, mostly unused. Hannah glimpsed dust-sheets and four-poster beds.

Margaret stopped. 'This is Lady Foxcroft's private sitting room,' she whispered. 'This is where we can hear them talking when we're higher up. We're on the same level now. This is where they come when they don't want to be overheard or disturbed, even by the servants.'

The passage narrowed again for the chimney breast, and Hannah stooped to put her eye carefully to the nearest slit. She was looking through the back of the fireplace and saw a charmingly modern room, furnished entirely in the latest fashion with green and gold hangings.

'It's empty now.' Margaret was disappointed. 'They were here when I set off to find you. But you argued too long, as you always do.'

'We can wait a little while. They may come back.' But Hannah doubted it. Lady Foxcroft on her own, maybe; but it was hardly likely that both their gaolers would appear to discuss their forthcoming actions so conveniently. She was only wishing to humour Margaret and demonstrate her belief in her. 'But we had better not stay too long. We may be missed.'

'They only come at meal times, and we have just eaten.'

'No, I have to answer more questions and make — well, a confession to Sir George.' Perhaps this lengthy absence from the room had not been a good idea. 'We must go back for now, but you have done well in discovering all this. I am sure it will be most helpful.'

'Yes, and now you can find a way for us to make our escape.'

'Possibly.' Hannah did not want to sound discouraging, but Lady Foxcroft's building work seemed to have prevented that. And if they did emerge in one of these lower rooms, assuming they could somehow open the hidden doors, they would have to make their way through the rest of the house, avoiding the legion of servants Lady Foxcroft considered appropriate for elegant living. Hannah could not see how any of this could be possible. 'I must go back.'

Margaret pulled a face but followed her. 'You left your door open a crack as I showed you, didn't you?'

'Yes.'

'When you have answered your questions, can we come here again? We will hear them discussing what you have said and what they really think.'

'Yes, that's a good idea.'

Margaret paused at her door, thinking. 'Hannah, what did you mean when you said you had to make a confession?'

Hannah sighed. 'Sir George has misunderstood things, or is pretending to. He says that you came here to get away from me because you were terrified of my mistreatment of you, and thought you might suffer the unfortunate fate of Violet and now Lavinia — because you have accused me of their murders.'

Margaret's face was pale with horror. 'Oh, Hannah, I never meant that. How can he think it? I don't understand.'

'I know. You ran away because you were angry with me, and Sir George has understood very well indeed and twisted whatever you may have said to suit his own purposes.'

'I should have been more careful in what I said. I am so sorry.'

'Being careful in what you say has never come easily to you; I know that. It is not your fault. And those who love you do so just as you are, and me most of all. Never change.'

Margaret shook her head. 'You have

been a wonderful sister to me. I have not appreciated you as I should.'

'And I have not tried to understand you as I should, and made allowances, when saying and doing the right thing is hard for you. Never mind; when we get out of here safely, everything will be different. I promise.' They hugged each other, difficult as that was in the confined space. 'And now we must go back. I will make this nonsensical confession with new strength, knowing how Sir George has lied.'

Margaret smiled. 'And then you will find a way out of here. I know you will.'

12

When Margaret returned to join her at last, Hannah was sitting quietly on her chair, still feeling shaken after her interview with Sir George.

He had seemed almost kindly at first. 'Why is your sister so afraid of you?' he asked.

He must already know that Margaret was not, but Hannah explained the difficulties of their relationship as if to someone who had never met them before.

His expression became more severe with every word she spoke. 'I have to take your sister's testimony seriously, with the utmost concern. Who better than she to understand your true nature? And I have to draw the most unpleasant conclusions.'

She stared into his face. He could not possibly believe what he was saying. 'Regarding?'

'The deaths of two of your pupils. I am led to the inevitable conclusion that you were responsible.'

'They were placed in my care by their parents, so yes, I must take full responsibility for what happened to them.'

'You are pretending to misunderstand me.' He sighed. 'If you are capable of causing such terror within your innocent, trusting and vulnerable younger sister, I consider that you would be quite capable of these killings.'

'No.' Hannah shook her head. 'I would not. And, Sir George, what possible reason could I have for doing these terrible things?'

'Ah!' He sat back a little as if producing an indisputable fact. 'Jealousy, naturally.'

'Jealousy?' Hannah stared at him in disbelief. 'Of what? That does not make any sense.'

'My dear, the whole village knew of your sad disappointment when I brought home my new wife. It was based on

248

flimsy foundations, I am afraid, for I never made any such promise to you.'

'Or to my father?'

'He chose to misunderstand our casual conversations. He knew I must seek a wife with financial considerations in mind. But as I said, I can see how he led you to expect otherwise, and how you were devastated when you discovered the realities of the situation.'

Hannah realised she had fallen into his trap. She said, 'I may have experienced a certain regret at the time, but that is all over and done now. Indeed, I am content with my position with my school, and I rejoice in your happiness.'

'So content you must give dinner parties for the express purpose of seeking recommendations for further pupils? You were already on shaky ground before you performed these dreadful acts. Driven by anger and jealousy, as I said.'

'You have not told me why I should

have been jealous of either Violet or Lavinia.'

'Because, my dear, they had both made unfortunate and inappropriate advances to me.'

She went white. 'To you?' Was Sir George, then, the father of Violet's child? If so, once Hannah admitted she knew of Violet's child, she would be sealing her fate — and Margaret's too. Sir George would be unable to let them go.

He rose to his feet. 'I see by your face I have hit upon the truth of it. Thank you, Hannah. That will be all for now.'

'And what next?' Hannah said, trying to regain her wits. 'If you are to accuse me of murder, surely I must stand trial?' There would be her opportunity. She could speak out against him, voicing what he had all but admitted to her.

'That is the usual procedure in such cases.' He nodded and went out.

No, it was all too obvious. She would never be allowed to stand trial. He could not take the risk when he did not know how much she knew and what she would say.

Margaret was only a few moments behind him in coming through the panelling. 'They are there now. We must go down to the lower corridor where we can both hear. They will be discussing what he thinks about what you said.'

'Yes, I am sure they will,' Hannah said, unable to sound optimistic.

'He will be telling Lady Foxcroft what he is going to do next.' Margaret turned quickly, scanning Hannah's face anxiously. 'Though you did tell him I didn't say any of those dreadful things — and didn't mean what I *did* say, didn't you?'

'Yes, I did. And I am sure he believed me. But I fear he is choosing to pretend he doesn't.'

There was no further opportunity for speech or they would risk being heard. They crouched by the slit in the wall together. Hannah tried placing one eye to the aperture, but Sir George and his wife were seated away from the empty fireplace, in spite of the chill of the day. Fortunately they had not ordered a fire to be lit in there, for whatever reason. But all Hannah could see was part of Sir George's back and his left arm. Lady Foxcroft was out of her vision entirely.

Lady Foxcroft was saying, 'You have to. It is apparent that she knows far too much.'

'No. I cannot do it. I cannot kill in cold blood.'

Hannah put a warning hand over Margaret's lips to hide her gasp. She was shocked too, even though it was what she had begun to expect. What else could he do?

Lady Foxcroft gave a contemptuous exclamation. 'Where is the difference? You have killed twice already.'

'Be quiet. I have told you how it was. Yes, I attacked Violet when she was trying to blackmail me. You know this — how the little slut was trying to claim I was the father of the child she carried.

I received a note from her and went over to the school that night, on foot, when the snow stopped. I was filled with fury, I admit it. I had my hands around her throat — and then sense prevailed and I flung her from me and she knocked her head against the wall. But even so, she was not dead when I left her. She was weeping and making a ridiculous fuss about how she did not know what to do. I was tempted to silence her, but I did not. She was alive when I left her.'

'I suppose this is what one takes on in marrying into the gentry,' Lady Foxcroft said. 'Although you would be wise to remember my father holds the purse and would not be pleased at your treatment of me. But what about the other one?'

'An accident. She slipped. Yes, I was with her. She was a close friend of Violet's. She knew everything. She thought she could continue with Violet's blackmail attempt. She soon discovered her mistake, and we are well rid of her.'

Lady Foxcroft sniffed loudly. 'Accidents, as you say. No doubt. But what are we to do with our prisoners? Are they also to meet with suitable accidents? You may have brought Lavinia's body back here, but there is plenty of room yet by the stream, in that unstable bank, to conceal a further two bodies, and to make a better job of it this time. When they are eventually discovered, months or even years hence, we shall be as shocked and horrified as everyone else.'

To Hannah's horror, Sir George was silent, as if considering the plan. Surely he could not? And *had* the other deaths been accidents, as he claimed? 'Very clever, I'm sure,' he said. 'But too much of a risk.'

'We have to do something. Already that minister could be on his way here. They have no relatives to miss them, but *he* will not accept Hannah's disappearance. He will be a constant thorn in our sides. Are we to dispose of him too? And half the village with him?'

'He will be no problem at all. I can have words with various contacts I have in the hierarchy of his church and cause him to be moved elsewhere.'

'Oh, Sir George! Sometimes you are the most complete fool. It is all too obvious that the minister is in love with Hannah. He will not give up easily.'

Now it was Hannah's turn to hide a gasp. Margaret was smiling and nodding at her. This was surely not true. Did everyone think it but her?

Sir George seemed as surprised as she was. 'Are you sure? Well, I suppose women have an eye for these things, particularly when they do not have enough to occupy themselves. It's a pity he did not think to offer for her earlier. All of these problems might have been avoided.'

'So — what are you going to do?'

His voice was suddenly louder, and Hannah could no longer see him in the chair, as if he was walking about at this end of the room. 'You have given me an idea that would be much more acceptable. I believe there are two alternatives I can offer to Hannah. Either would work well. Yes, I believe I have something there, and no time like the present. I shall go and put them to her straightaway.'

Hannah recoiled from the slit in horror. Would they have time to get back? For once Margaret was reacting just as quickly. Behind them, they could hear Lady Foxcroft crying shrilly, 'Wait, what alternatives? What are you going to do? I demand that you tell me.'

Hannah had never thought, as they sped along the passageways and back up the stairs, that she would ever feel so grateful to Lady Foxcroft. She hoped and prayed Sir George's wife would delay him sufficiently.

They came to Margaret's room. Margaret was swiftly through the hidden door, and Hannah had only to reach her own. Her heart seemed to be beating more loudly than her footsteps, but she had done it; she was there before him. She made herself close the panel slowly and softly, all the while listening for his approach. She sat down, hands demurely in her lap. Would Sir George notice a heightened colour or the way her chest was heaving? Could all this be accounted for by the distress of being confined here?

The door opened and she looked up, half-expecting to see the evidence of Sir George's villainy in his face and to recoil from it. But he looked calm and collected and no different from usual. He said, 'Good. I am pleased to find you sitting quietly.' He seemed to be nodding approval. 'Sadly, your sister could not understand our higher motivation at first and railed and screamed against our kindness. But you will be pleased to hear she is now comfortable and content.'

Hannah said belatedly, 'I am so pleased to hear you say so.' Of course, she should have asked about Margaret sooner. Why hadn't she thought of that? 'How is she? I demand to know. I must see her.'

'I am afraid she does not wish to see you. Most regrettable, I know.' He shook his head sadly. 'But you can hardly be surprised after the serious accusations she has made against you. The evidence is indisputable. I have considered your version of events carefully and can draw no other conclusion.'

There seemed no purpose in pleading with him. She said quietly, 'Am I to stand trial?'

'No. I have decided against that. In consideration of the long friendship between myself and your father, I cannot publicly besmirch his family name and reputation.'

'Thank you.' He was pausing while Hannah waited to hear the solutions he had thought of during his conversation with his wife. She clenched her fingers into her palms to try and hide her impatience.

'Therefore, I have thought of an alternative. I can offer you an advantageous marriage, involving a move to the colonies. It is better than anything you could have expected.'

Hannah's head jerked back in surprise. 'A marriage? I suppose . . . Yes. Many people would think so.' She could not hide her amazement. 'I wonder you did not consider it before, when Margaret and I were at our wits' end as to how to support ourselves.'

Sir George said smoothly, 'The opportunity has only just arisen — a wealthy cousin who is in need of a wife to order his entertaining on his slave plantation. The position needs a woman of good sense and breeding.'

'Yes, I see. Is this a cousin of yours or your wife's? Although that would not affect my answer.' Hannah was too angry to think clearly.

'Do not answer too quickly and dismiss this out of hand. There you would enjoy greater status than here; wealth and position. Here, you would be a convicted murderess.'

She had to say it. 'But I might not be convicted. I am innocent.'

'I am the law here, Hannah. The trial would be in my keeping.'

'Would it, though? Surely a capital trial would take place with a judge and jury? Somewhere like York.'

'All the judges are known to me. They would take my advice. Please consider your options with care.'

She said slowly, 'And Margaret?'

'I am sure you and I together may persuade her to forgive you and therefore accompany you. Think how she would benefit from such a position.'

And the unspoken option which lay between them — disposing of them both in some unspecified manner — was no choice at all. Hannah supposed she would have to accept, however she felt about it. 'I don't know,' she said carefully. 'To achieve a safe and peaceful future where I would no longer have to make all the decisions for our well-being — which has been a heavy burden; to hand over all such responsibility to a husband . . . That is most tempting.

But still, I need time to consider.'

He frowned. 'I had hoped for an answer immediately. I am disappointed by the comments you have already made. I do not feel you show true gratitude. And while you delay, my cousin may well find someone else.'

She saw it at once — they would never reach this cousin. They would make their farewells and leave, waving their handkerchiefs through carriage windows, and never be seen again — if the cousin even existed. This choice was no choice. Hannah hoped the realisation did not show in her face. She put a faltering hand to her brow. 'I do not know what to say in the face of such generosity. This is too much to take in all at once. Such an opportunity. I beg you, please give me time to consider it further.'

Sir George consulted his watch. 'I am not an unreasonable man, I think. One cannot expect the female mind to make swift decisions. Shall we say nine o'clock tomorrow morning?'

She tried to look as if she might be about to swoon. 'Thank you. Thank you so much.'

'Without fail, then.' As he stood up, Hannah tried to interpret his expression. Pleasure? Triumph? If she had married Sir George, she would not have been able to play his Lady Macbeth, while Lady Foxcroft seemed well suited to that role. She shuddered.

No time for that. She crept to the door and listened for his departing steps. She must talk to Margaret at once. Should she have mentioned that to Sir George? Yes, she should have asked to consult her sister. Insisted upon it, even. It was difficult to try and decide how she would have behaved; she hoped she had been convincing. Too late now.

She opened the door and squeezed along the passageway. Margaret's room was empty. Where was she? No need to ask. As Hannah reached the spiral stairway, Margaret was coming up. Hannah allowed a brief smile; they were becoming accustomed to this strange abode.

'Quickly!' Margaret hissed. 'You are so slow. They are talking about us.'

Hannah nodded and once again followed Margaret to where they could hear. There was no need this time to place their ears near the slit in the wall. Lady Foxcroft was shrieking in anger.

'You did what? Why did you not consult me? We cannot be sure your cousin Walter will control them. They will be free to spread lies about you. We shall never be free of them.'

'You are quite wrong, my dear. You did not meet Walter before he left, but I have every faith in him. Once they are with Walter, we shall have no further problems.'

Hannah felt a chilling of her blood at the ruthlessness of his tone.

Lady Foxcroft was walking up and down in her agitation, her wide skirts swishing as she turned. 'So you say. I trust we do not. But what if she refuses? What are you going to do then? In my opinion, you have given her far too long to consider it. She may come up with all kinds of objections through the hours of darkness.'

'I am sure she will come to the only sensible decision. The alternative is too bleak, and she has to consider her sister. But this is their whole future after all.'

'And they are lucky to have one. You must demand their decision by this evening; and if you are not bold enough to tell her of this new condition, then I shall. Now.'

A door slammed. Hannah was momentarily frozen, hardly understanding the significance of Lady Foxcroft's words. 'Quickly,' she hissed. 'I must get back before them.'

Margaret was complaining as Hannah pushed past, hardly noticing how she was grazing her knuckles on the rough stone. Margaret's complaints echoed up the stairs after her. 'You can't do it. You'll never get there. Let them think we've disappeared.'

Hannah was panting as she reached

the stairs. This way was longer, of course; she had had to go in the wrong direction to reach the stairs before retracing her steps along the upper passage. Lady Foxcroft's way would be much more direct. But Lady Foxcroft would not be running. And why had Sir George not stopped her? Why had he not argued with her?

Hannah was almost there. She should be able to see the faint gap in the stone where she had carefully left the door not quite closed. Surely she should have reached it by now? No, she must have passed it. Had she forgotten to leave it open? She slid her fingers along the stone. Yes, here was the ridge where it should be, where wood met stone.

It was closed. She scrabbled desperately at the door, tearing her nails, ignoring the sear of pain.

Sir George's voice seemed very close. 'But how is this, my dear? Where is our caged bird?' He sounded almost amused.

The door was shut. Hannah could

not get back. And would not want to, now.

'I knew it,' Lady Foxcroft cried. 'I knew it should have been done at once. Perhaps now you will listen to me. They have escaped and we are lost.'

Hannah was thinking rapidly. There must be a way. What about Margaret's door? But she had already passed that without seeing it. That was shut too. Perhaps they could wait for a servant to come into one of the rooms and call out to them for help; get them to take a message to Tom or Millie — or Mr Woodward.

Margaret was behind her. 'My door is shut. I have been in and out a dozen times since coming here. I never make that mistake.'

'Perhaps a servant has been in and closed it.'

'They could hardly see it.'

'I will think of something.' Hannah turned, too sharply, and felt her sleeve catch and tear. What must they look like, covered in dust and cobwebs, and now with her hands bleeding? It was fortunate that Sir George had noticed nothing amiss when he was speaking to her.

She felt a shiver of foreboding. 'Well,' she said briskly, 'we must find another way out. We must search every inch of the walls and find a way into one of the other rooms.'

It would at least be something to occupy their minds and stave off panic. She must not allow Margaret to consider what might happen if there was no way out. She must not allow herself to consider it either. 'This network of passages is so cleverly done; I am sure there must have been an escape route for the priests if they heard the searchers becoming too close.'

'Yes,' Margaret said suddenly. 'There *is* something. I always thought so. There was another opening further along, and I could see how it opened from this side. But as a child, my fingers could not stretch far enough. With two of us, we may do it.'

13

'Can you remember where it was?' Hannah hardly dared hope of it.

'Oh, yes. I never forget things like that.' Her fingers brushed confidently over the stones. 'Here it is. Just with a wider gap. I can reach the catches myself now.'

At last! Hannah had little hope in Margaret's solution, but the door opened easily and well. Strange that the passage should end in a door. This must be a way out. Would it lead to another stair? Hannah felt like weeping with relief.

They peered forwards into darkness. There was far less light here than in the rest of the passages, but gradually Hannah found she could see through the gloom. There were no stairs in the far corner. This seemed merely to be a room, although they had more space here.

She could hear voices again. Where were they, Lady Foxcroft was saying. 'That will do now. You might have known we would need a fire in here. It should have been lit earlier.'

Hannah could imagine a servant scurrying away. Sir George's voice boomed out nearby. 'I shall sit here and reflect for a few moments. There are some legal works here in the library that I need to consult.'

There was a knocking sound close to Hannah's head, and immediately the room was filled with the customary dim light as at least three slits were revealed. Hannah heard him move away and cautiously placed her eye to one of them. Of course! They were now behind the library. By great good fortune, Sir George had selected the very books that aligned with the slits. And they needed some good fortune, she reflected; this was not before time.

Next to her, Margaret gave a muffled scream, broken off as Hannah pressed a hand to her mouth. 'Ssh.' She could feel

Margaret's shoulders shaking. 'Is it a rat?'

'Worse,' Margaret hissed.

The sliver of light shone like the beam of a lamp, illuminating something against the rear wall: a huddled shape, wrapped in dust coloured cloth. 'It's a body,' Margaret breathed.

'Surely not.' Hannah wanted to be reassuring, but she could see at once that Margaret was right. 'And dead for a very long time.' Hannah tried to sound matter-of-fact. By a huge effort of will, she managed to control the trembling in her limbs. 'It will not trouble us. It will be one of the priests who was concealed here.'

'And why is he here still?' Margaret demanded. 'What happened to him? Why could he not get out?'

'Perhaps he was old and died naturally.'

'Or the family here had to leave suddenly and there was no one to bring him food. And no one to let him out. And that means we are still trapped

270

too.' Margaret's eyes were wide and fearful. In another moment, she might lose all control and give them away. Hannah could read the signs.

'We don't know that. If he died of any number of natural causes, the family would know removing him for burial would give them away.' Was this convincing? However, Margaret seemed calmer now. Hannah hoped Sir George had not heard any of their ill-considered exchange.

No; here was Lady Foxcroft again. 'Ah, Sir George. Why are you sitting here in the cold with the fire so low? Let me call Meadows to revive it a little if you must sit here.' She was speaking in a slow and measured fashion and in carrying tones, quite unlike her usual shrill and hurried manner.

'It seems you were correct, my dear. We do have certain problems that must be addressed. No need to call Meadows; he will only disturb my thoughts. I will see to it myself. The fires in this room never light easily and tend to smoke; the chimney breast is not at all conveniently placed. I have never known why. But there is no need to be concerned for my health on that score, the smoke can exit elsewhere, rather than out into the library here. And see, my dear, what I will now demonstrate to you within the fireplace itself. If I adjust this most cunning arrangement of shutters, the smoke will not trouble us at all.'

There was a scraping sound; and before them, lower down, another opening appeared. At the same time, the entrance door gave an ominous click.

'I am glad we have caused the fire to be lit today,' Sir George said. 'For I am very much afraid we have rats in the walls again. I am certain I heard them scrabbling in there only a few moments ago.'

Lady Foxcroft gave a little scream. 'Rats. Oh, no. You must do something.'

'There is no need for you to worry. The smoke will soon deal with them.

The whole system has been very cleverly designed.'

He was right, Hannah saw. Small gusts of smoke were puffing into the room.

Margaret was already coughing. 'We will die here, and no one will know it.'

'I think we will have to declare ourselves,' Hannah said. What else could she do? She could not risk her sister's life, even if she was willing to endanger her own. 'Help,' she called. 'We are trapped here. Douse the fire, I beg you.'

'Did you hear a strange sound?' Lady Foxcroft asked.

'It is only the rats squealing before they expire. Pay no attention. Troublesome, I know, but inevitable. Leave this to me if it distresses you.'

Hannah sank against the wall. No wonder everything had seemed so easy. How could she have been so blind? Sir George had lived here since childhood. If Margaret could find the secret ways as a visitor, he would have had far greater opportunity. And now he had made good use of his further knowledge. *He knew all along,* Hannah thought bitterly. *We have been enticed here, like rats in a trap indeed.*

'Sir George, Sir George!' Margaret shouted. By the library wall, they could scarcely breathe.

Hannah pulled herself up to cross the room. 'Come over to me, where the air is still clear.'

'But we are going to die here. Why does he not answer?'

'He knows we're here,' Hannah said. 'It is all part of his plan. Hush. Maybe our best hope lies in convincing him we are dead already. Perhaps he will then control the fire.'

'No, no. He won't. He can't.' Margaret was screaming as she banged on the wall.

'Stop that,' Hannah croaked. 'It won't help us.'

Margaret was weeping now, but she followed Hannah to the other side of the room; though strangely the banging went on, muffled and distant. Hannah turned her head, frowning. Was the smoke giving her delusions? No, of course not. They must be above the front door.

'Who can that be, Lady Foxcroft?' Sir George cried. 'Someone come to disturb us? But no matter, for I think our rats are subsiding.' And now he was addressing the butler. 'Ah, yes. Please show the minister in here.'

'In here? Are you mad?' Lady Foxcroft hardly waited for the door to close behind Meadows.

'No, indeed. I know what I am doing. Have no fear. And I am merely adding a little game of my own to my overall plan. I cannot resist it. We do not need to look far for the reason for his visit. He is seeking and searching for the lady who holds his heart. Most touching.'

How dare he? Hannah thought. *Making a game of Mr Woodward's feelings. And he is quite wrong. I cannot think how he has arrived at that conclusion. Surely I would know if Mr*

Woodward felt that way about me? Her heart felt empty. *I only wish he did.*

And now she had missed what Sir George was saying. Lady Foxcroft said, 'You mean you will express your regret at not knowing where Hannah may be? And send him on his way, all the time with her not six feet away?'

'Exactly.'

'But he is like a terrier. He will never give up.'

'He will have no choice, for now, but to be on his way. And soon the two bodies will be found, as with our original plan, overcome by the disastrous landslip that also took Lavinia.'

'That means putting too much trust in the servants, in my opinion.'

'It does not need more than the two who have already shown their loyalty and silence to me and will continue to do, so because I pay them well.'

'And if someone else offers more?'

'A Nonconformist minister has no money. And who else would take the trouble? It matters not. This is what we shall do, with your agreement or without it.'

'Oh, you have it. I am not disputing the deed itself, merely the best way of going about it. But if anything goes wrong and you are discovered, I shall deny all knowledge of it.'

'I expected no less. I have no illusions where you are concerned, my dear. Ah, Reverend Woodward. It is always good to see you. Come and sit by the fire.'

The smoke was rising lazily; by the chimney breast it had reached head height. Margaret was seated against the wall as far away as possible, no longer worrying about the nearness of what was indisputably a body. There was still light showing through one of the slits. Sir George had not replaced one of the books.

Hannah felt her way back and placed her mouth by the slit. 'Mr Woodward!' she called. The effort made her cough.

Near at hand, Sir George was rattling the fire tongues, covering her poor effort to call for help. 'It is a cold, dreary day. A good fire is essential, do you not agree?'

'I cannot stay, Sir George. I am urgently seeking Miss Hannah. She set out in search of Miss Margaret, and no one seems to know where she may have gone.'

'I am sorry to hear that. Dear, dear. I can gather some servants and mount a search if you wish. These grounds have been sadly neglected since her father died and contain many treacherous spots, particularly in this weather.'

'Good. Thank you. But I will not wait. I shall continue alone, and you may follow with your party.'

'Wait just a moment. You have heard of the sad death of Lavinia, one of her pupils? We retrieved her body a few hours ago. She, too, had been missing all night. I will ask if any of my servants noticed anything untoward when they were out there. It will not take a moment and may help in your search.'

Where had that other slit been? Hannah felt along the wall once more with fingers so grazed that they felt numb. Here, she was certain of it. A slit she had not noticed before. Because it was not a slit; it was another door opening out into the library.

She heard the main door to the library closing. Had Sir George gone? Was the minister now alone? She had not the strength to wonder why Sir George might leave him in this way; she had to attract Mr Woodward's attention before their room became totally filled with smoke. At least it seemed intermittent in the way it puffed and stopped.

Margaret, over by the body, was moving again. 'Mr Woodward!' Hannah called.

'You need to tap with something,' Margaret said. She joined Hannah by the door. 'Use this.' She pressed an object into Hannah's hand. It was hard and round, made of metal. A pocket watch. Hannah banged on the door and at last he heard her.

'Hannah? Where are you?'

'In a room in the wall. You can open the door from your side.'

Blessedly, he was swift to understand her instructions. At last the door opened and she and Margaret fell, more than stepped, into the library.

'Hannah!' Woodward caught her in his arms. 'Are you all right?'

She was coughing almost too much to speak. 'I am now.' But how many minutes more before it would have been too late?

'And Margaret?' he said gently. 'How about you?'

'Hannah made me go to the back of the room, by the dead priest. I wasn't in the smoke as much as she was.' Margaret gave her a look of gratitude. 'She saved me.'

'We are not saved yet,' Hannah said quickly. 'Sir George was hoping to tell you I had accepted an offer to marry a cousin of his in the colonies, to avoid being put on trial for the murders of Violet and Lavinia.'

'We heard him talking,' Margaret

said, 'through the wall. I found the way. We heard his plan.'

'We must get away from here,' Hannah said.

'We shall,' Woodward said. 'Sir George is not the only one to have a plan. Never fear; we will get out of this.'

'Sir George will be coming back. We must hurry.'

Too late. The door was flung open and Sir George was already there, seemingly not the slightest disconcerted. 'Ah, minister. You have discovered our guests, I see.'

'And discovered what you had planned for them. How could you ever hope I would believe such a nonsensical story?' Woodward was edging round so the women were standing behind him. 'That Hannah would agree to leave here to marry a man she had never met — and all to avoid some ludicrous accusations for which you had no evidence?'

'Not at all. Hannah has indeed met my cousin Walter. Have you not?' Sir George was smiling. 'He has been staying with us for some time now. I assume he is happy with his accommodation, for he has never complained.'

Hannah cried, 'No, I have not. I do not know this cousin Walter.'

'Well, your hand gives the lie to that. You are holding his pocket watch.'

Hannah almost dropped it. 'But . . . I didn't . . . Margaret, where did you find this?'

Margaret's voice was shaking. 'I found it in there, on the body. I was looking for something to help us.'

'But I thought . . . I assumed it would be a priest, trapped here in the time of priest's holes and religious discrimination.'

'I doubt whether seventeenth-century priests had pocket watches,' said Sir George, smiling. 'An excellent display of logic.'

Woodward said briskly, 'You knew he was there. I can only assume you killed him, or had him killed. Since he was supposedly on his way to a new life, he would not be missed.'

'His death was unfortunate — and unintentional.'

Hannah was trying to warn Woodward with her eyes. If anything, their situation was now worse than ever. Knowing this, they could never be allowed to leave here alive. And now Mr Woodward was in the same situation. She said quickly, 'I am sure you did not mean to hurt him. Or maybe he suffered a sudden apoplexy? As so often happens.'

Woodward was steadfastly ignoring her warning. 'No. I believe you to be guilty of murder, Sir George. And concealing the body for — how many years — since your unfortunate cousin died?'

Sir George was still calm; a calm that made Hannah all the more fearful. He turned to speak to her. 'I believe this young man, though principled and worthy I am sure, should be careful in his accusations. Because, Hannah, I am afraid your father was heavily involved in the circumstances surrounding Walter's death.'

'My father?'

'Indeed. And if the minister here has any kind of feeling for you, he should surely not involve you in the ensuing embarrassment and stigma if the truth became known.'

Hannah armed herself against the shock. 'I do not believe you. You can say anything you like against our father because he is not here to defend himself. I consider that underhand.'

Woodward said, 'It is. Can you justify your accusations?'

Sir George shrugged. 'Hannah's father was a good friend of mine and a frequent visitor. We would play cards in the evenings. And when my cousin Walter stayed with me, on his way to Liverpool to take ship, the game became all the more interesting. He had a large amount of money with him, naturally, and was eager to raise the stakes to increase the funds he would carry to his new venture. Walter was always a fool, however, and a poor card player to boot. He lost, and carried on losing — and then accused us of cheating him. Naturally I could not let such an accusation pass unchallenged.'

'You fought a duel?'

'Of a kind. There and then. Walter would not wait for the formalities of seconds, et cetera, as he needed to be off at first light. I have to admit that it was more of a scuffle than a duel. But he was no better at fighting than he had been at cards — and within minutes, he lay dead.' He put a hand to his brow, shaking his head sadly. 'I was stricken with grief. He was a relative, after all. I did not know what to do. But Hannah, your father kept his head. It was he who pointed out no one need know of Walter's death. I could rise early and declare I had witnessed his departure, if anyone should ask, which hardly seemed likely. And he helped me to hide the body in the secret room, to be forgotten.'

'What of the money?' Woodward said coldly.

Sir George shrugged. 'Walter had no further need of it.'

'And both of *you* certainly did,' Woodward said.

Hannah frowned. On their father's death, there had been only an inheritance of unwelcome debts. 'Are you saying you bought my father's silence?'

'Your father was an honourable man. He would not take the money. No, he asked for something else — and I think you might guess what it was. He wanted me as a husband for his elder daughter. I had to agree. Although it was not something I had ever thought of or planned. I was older than you after all, Hannah. But I liked you well enough.'

Hannah felt the pain of the shame that washed over her. 'But there was never any formal proposal. My father hinted at it, I recall. And then . . . '

'And then your father died,' Sir George continued smoothly. 'And there was no need to continue with this somewhat distasteful arrangement. Indeed, it would not have been at all practicable financially. There was no doubt about that.'

Margaret said suddenly, 'Our father's death was very convenient for you.'

Sir George laughed. 'Yes, it was. But I am in no way responsible for that.'

Hannah said quickly, 'No, no, I am sure Margaret did not mean anything of the kind.'

'Yes, I did. Why not, when he has killed so many other people?'

'That is not an opinion I would repeat, if I were you,' Sir George said.

'No, I'm sure you wouldn't. But what difference will it make? You have killed so many, you won't stop at three more. I know that, if Hannah does not.'

'Margaret, please.' When it had not been spoken aloud between them and was based solely on what they had overheard, Hannah had thought there might be a chance to leave here alive.

'We would be missed,' Woodward said calmly. 'Various people will come searching for us.'

'Too late to be of any practical use to you, I am afraid. By then you will have met with an unfortunate accident of some sort. I will join in the search, naturally, and show great distress when the bodies are discovered.'

'You misunderstand me, Sir George,' the minister said. 'There will be little need for an actual search. People know where I am.'

'What people?' Sir George said lazily. 'You are bluffing, Woodward. There is no one with greater legal authority than I in this locality.'

He was interrupted by a loud knocking and pounding on the main door; so loud that it could have been in the room with them.

Reverend Woodward said quietly, 'I believe that will be Sir Joseph Steading with the local militia.'

14

Sir George rose to his feet. 'Anything you say will be your word against mine. Sir Joseph thinks most highly of me.' He turned to the door. 'Ah, Sir Joseph. You are always most welcome. I willingly answered your summons the other day but was told there had been an unfortunate mistake.' He glanced around the room. 'And I see you have brought armed companions. We were about to instigate a wider search following the most unfortunate attacks here, so their presence will be most welcome.'

Sir Joseph, tall and spare, gave him a stern look. 'I am afraid we are unlikely to be searching any further than these walls, Sir George. I have spoken to a number of people, and consider it unfortunate you were the one to begin the investigations into the first death.

You did not follow correct procedures. I wish I could have intervened sooner. No matter, however, as through the timely intervention of the Nonconformist minister here, I believe I have arrived in time.'

Sir George shook his head in amusement. 'An excitable young man, a newcomer to the area, as your main informant — and doubtless you will be subjected to a lurid account by these two hysterical women also. And these are your witnesses?'

'No, there are others.' Sir Joseph paused. Perhaps he had expected Sir George to crumble in the face of a higher authority, and his relaxed confidence was giving him cause to doubt. 'I think we should sit privately while you give me your account of all that has occurred.'

No! Hannah thought. He must not be allowed to do that. He would talk himself out of it.

But there was someone, it seemed, who did not share Hannah's opinion.

Without warning, the library door opened and Lady Foxcroft stood there, her face pale with anger. 'I told you what would happen! I warned you.'

'My dear,' Sir George said, striding across the room to her and seizing her arm, 'there is no need for alarm. Your entrance is inopportune. Please be calm.'

But Lady Foxcroft's fury did not make any provision for calm. Without realising her husband might indeed, left to himself, extricate himself from his predicament, she cried, 'I told you I would not support you in this wickedness. You must not think that any of it had anything to do with me, Sir Joseph.'

'As his wife, you are not obliged to give evidence against him,' Sir Joseph explained kindly.

'But I will. My father chose badly for me, I see that now. I have been used and put upon, and I want only to be rid of him. I shall tell you everything I know.'

Sir Joseph nodded. 'Thank you. If

that is what you wish to do.'

Sir George shook his head. 'And I am to be condemned on the testimony of a crowd of women and a dissenting minister? It will not do, Sir Joseph. I protest most strongly at the correctness of it.'

'You shall have your turn, of course. But first I will hear your wife. Do we have another room, Lady Foxcroft? And the ladies and the Reverend Woodward may wait in another, while one of the soldiers will wait with you, Sir George. This is merely correct procedure.'

'Do not leave him in this room,' Lady Foxcroft said. 'This house is riddled with secret tunnels and passages. He will be off through them.'

By the look on Sir George's face, he had been entertaining the same thought. Sir Joseph said, 'Whatever you suggest, madam.'

Hannah felt weak with relief as servants showed them to a small parlour and they could at last sit quietly, although she would not rest properly until she was back at the school. She had already been away too long.

Sir Joseph was brisk and efficient, and his questions had a searching intelligence. All the same, the whole took what seemed like hours. Woodward carefully opened the door leading out to the main hallway. 'I am sure Sir Joseph will tell us what he has decided, but I prefer to hear for myself.'

The militia were being gathered in the hall again and obviously surrounding Sir George as a military escort. 'They are arresting him,' Margaret whispered. 'I'm glad of it. But you know, I think he would have escaped that if Lady Foxcroft had not been so disloyal. If I had a husband, I wouldn't do that. And neither would you, Hannah. If he had married you as he promised Father, you would not betray him, whatever he had done.'

'Hush, Margaret. These are private matters.' She glanced at Mr Woodward, who seemed to be pretending he had not heard, but had a smile in his eyes.

'Oh, the whole village knew it,' Margaret said. 'But then, Sir George did not turn out well, so it was best you did not take him. And it leaves you free to marry someone far more suitable.' She gave a significant nod and moved to the window.

Woodward was nodding too. 'Wise words, Margaret. Ah, I think they are leaving. A moment.' He slipped through the door. 'Sir Joseph, will you be needing us further?'

'Thank you, no. Not at present. Although I am afraid you at least will have to be called when this sad case comes to trial. We may be able to spare the ladies.'

Hannah left the room to stand beside him. 'Indeed not, Sir Joseph. If you need my testimony, I shall be more than willing to give it.' She glanced at Sir George. He was pale and still, standing stiffly, all the lazy confidence and arrogant bluster gone. 'I am sorry that this should have happened, but it is important that justice is served.'

'I think we may leave also,' Mr Woodward said quietly. 'Unless you feel we should take leave of Lady Foxcroft?'

'I doubt if she would want us to. But I will just collect our cloaks and hats from the rooms where we were imprisoned.' Hannah turned and hurried up the stairs. It was easy to retrieve them, and Margaret's too. She could hear Sir Joseph and party going outside and the wheels of a small closed coach being brought round. She hesitated. The door to what was obviously Lady Foxcroft's small dressing room was open. Easier by far to leave without speaking to their hostess, if so she might be called.

The decision was taken for her. 'Miss Hannah. Come in here,' Lady Foxcroft said. 'Oh, do not worry. I am not going to hurt you in any way. I just want you to appreciate what you have done. See, from here we may watch a once proud man leaving his home in shackles. You have ruined everything he stood for.'

'I certainly have not. He made his own choices.'

'But you and your school. Without that in close proximity, there would have been no temptations. Men are always weak.'

Hannah shook her head. What was the point in arguing? Lady Foxcroft could hardly be counted on to hold a stable and logical opinion.

Suddenly, below them somewhere near the front door and out of their vision, came the noise of clattering hooves and raised voices. Hannah turned, thinking to go to the stairs to see what was happening, and Lady Foxcroft shrieked from the window, 'He is away! My husband is escaping!' Around the corner of the house and crossing the paddock rode Sir George, madly and without caution. Lady Foxcroft said, 'That is not one of our horses. Where has he found that?'

'It will be the one Mr Woodward borrowed,' Hannah murmured. 'He must not escape.' They would all be in danger. What kind of revenge might he seek?

'No!' Lady Foxcroft shrieked. 'Not that way, you fool!'

They had a clear view across the wide spread of the landscape. Sir George struck across to the west with the doctor's house looming on his right. Ahead the steep slope of the Cliff dropped away, down to the river in the valley.

Already the militia were following, mostly on foot but led by the two mounted men who would have been on hand to follow the coach. Hannah gasped, drawing the inevitable conclusion. Sir George must be intending to escape by taking the treacherous slope, where it was unlikely any of the others would dare to follow.

He was there. The horse, uncertain, seemed to pause; and then, spurred on, took the slope at a leap. The ground wobbled and shuddered beneath the pounding hooves — and as horse and rider landed, the whole of the slope crumbled and slid downwards, taking man and horse with it, turning and twisting in a horrendous distortion of forms and limbs.

'He is dead!' Lady Foxcroft cried. 'I saw it.' She turned to Hannah, who saw with a shock of horror that she was smiling. 'I am a widow.'

15

Mr Woodward said, 'I will escort you back, and then I will return here and see whether I can be of any assistance. I have spoken to Sir Joseph and he is in full agreement.'

'There is no need,' Hannah objected. 'We may surely walk across our own land safely.' She paused. 'Well, there is no danger now.'

'Of course there is need,' Margaret said. 'We accept your offer. It is most kind after the ordeals we have suffered.' She gave Hannah a nudge.

There was no purpose in arguing with Margaret when she had a notion in her head, whatever it might be. Hannah raised her eyebrows to Mr Woodward, who grinned back. She said, 'Very well. Thank you. And I do need to return as soon as possible. We have been absent for too long.'

She set out at a brisk pace, but Margaret was soon lagging behind. 'You two walk ahead,' she said bravely. 'I will keep you in sight. I am feeling dreadfully weary.'

Mr Woodward said gravely, 'I am sorry to hear that. Let me take your arm.'

'No, no,' Margaret said quickly. 'I am not *that* weary.'

He murmured to Hannah, 'I believe she wishes us to have an opportunity to be alone together.'

'I am sure I cannot think why,' Hannah said. She was beginning to feel tired also, too weary to cope with Margaret's games. And if she allowed herself to draw the obvious conclusion as to Margaret's aim, she would be overcome with embarrassment.

'That is a shame. I hoped you might. And Hannah, I have wanted to speak on many occasions over the last week but have been prevented by the tragic events surrounding us. Today even more so; it is hardly an appropriate time. But since your sister has mentioned it, might I have your permission to hope?'

Could he mean what she thought? It seemed too wonderful to be true. She was overwrought; allowing her imagination to flee away. 'If you mean . . . ' She stopped.

'Oh, Hannah!' Margaret cried, obviously not as far from hearing as she might have been. 'What are you thinking? Of course you must. He is the answer to everything — and anyway, your feelings for him are written plainly across your face.'

Hannah shook her head. 'I thought I was concealing my feelings.'

'Your sister knows you too well; I was not sure of them.'

Hannah took a deep breath. 'Before today, neither was I.'

They were approaching the school now. It was no longer a place of danger and uncertainty, as she had believed during the last few days; that was all behind them. She could reassure her pupils in good faith. As they rounded the last row of trees, however, they could see a coach bowling along the drive, travelling away from them. Two small hands waved from the window as the occupants caught sight of them.

'Who can that be?' Hannah murmured. She quickened her steps, almost running now, and with the other two beside her. She knew what had happened, of course. The news had got out, and at least one of the parents had reacted in the worst possible way.

She burst into the hall. The house seemed unusually quiet. There was not even the customary distant clatter of pans from the kitchen. The only sound was the rustle of Miss Hoyle's skirts as she came down the stairs, dressed for outdoors with her valise in her hand.

At least here was someone she could ask. Hannah regarded her with relief. 'Miss Hoyle, what is happening? Has someone left?'

'It is all accomplished,' Miss Hoyle said. 'I have completed what should have been done some time ago. The whole venture was ill-advised from the first.'

'What do you mean? What is accomplished?' But from the sinking Hannah could feel beneath her breast-bone, she thought she already knew.

'The girls have all gone. Mr Grey has kindly taken the Lee sisters together with Mary, and will deliver them safely on the way. He assured me the detour would be of no great inconvenience. He was pleased to be of assistance. They were the last.'

'Never mind Mr Grey. How has this happened? I left you in charge here.' Although if parents had arrived here demanding their daughters, there was little Miss Hoyle could do, Hannah supposed. 'You could at least have per-suaded them to wait until I returned.'

'And when was that to be? I did not know where you were, or if you were coming back. You could have been murdered yourself, for all I knew.'

Hannah opened her mouth to deny

it; but then, she and Margaret almost had been. That had been the intention. 'It cannot be helped, I suppose. I can understand their reaction. I am only surprised the parents heard of Violet's death so quickly.'

'Oh, Mr Grey was displeased he had not been notified sooner. He thanked me most profusely for my message. I sent Tom out with the messages, naturally. And he will not be the only person to thank me, I think.' She nodded. Hannah looked at her face closely for the first time. There was a strange light in her eyes. She began to wonder uneasily whether Miss Hoyle had been a fit person to be left in charge here.

Margaret had vanished along the corridor. Mr Woodward said quietly, 'Miss Hoyle, what did you mean? Who else will thank you, and why? I presume you do not mean the other parents.'

'Of course not. Ah, I believe I hear the trap that is to take myself and my trunk. I am to return to the hall, where

I shall receive the true gratitude due to me.'

She had not, of course, heard the dreadful news. Hannah said, 'Miss Hoyle, wait, please. There is something I must tell you.' Woodward put a hand on her arm and as she looked at him questioningly, shaking his head. It made little difference; Miss Hoyle had not even heard her, but was rattling on.

'You were all finely taken in, you see. Even Sir George could not be a party to it. When I first came here, when Lady Foxcroft declared she did not need old nursemaids around the place and cast me out and Sir George suggested I might be useful to you in your new venture, none of you knew the real motive for my arrival. But Lady Foxcroft instructed me well. Now that I have done exactly as she told me and the school is gone, Lady Foxcroft will be forever grateful to me. We both knew Sir George's weaknesses and the need to protect him from himself. But I have been ever alert, ever ready to act.'

'You have been the most loyal of servants,' Mr Woodward said. 'No one would ever doubt it. But it is unfortunate that Sir George must be held responsible for Violet's death.'

'Violet?' Miss Hoyle laughed. 'Not at all. He was angered when she told him she carried his child, knowing that Lady Foxcroft, in failing to produce children, might react very badly. He pushed her a little and she fell against the wall; even made as if to strangle her, but without any such intent. She was alive when he left, alive with the potential to be a severe nuisance. She came back inside; I had seen the whole from my window. When my dear boy is near, I always know; I always observe. I found her weeping by the outer door, and I took her to my room and let her weep and rail, and told her how she had made a bad mistake in telling him. Far better to allow their relationship to go on as it had. I offered her a draught that would dispose of the child. I watched her drink it with a touching gratitude and returned her to her bed.' She smiled, shaking her head. 'How easy it was to fool the devious little slut. I did not lie to her, however. The draught did indeed dispose of the child — and the mother also.'

'You killed Violet,' Hannah breathed.

'I had to protect him. I always have. It was by no means for the first time. And now they, with all their wealth and privilege, will protect me in return.' She smoothed her glove around her wrist, smiling.

'Not for the first time? Have you harmed anyone else?'

Miss Hoyle was suddenly angry. 'Sir George could do better than a match with you. He needed a bride with wealth and status, or else faced ruin. And yet your father had a hold over him, helping to conceal a cousin's body.'

'Cousin Walter!'

'Yes, that was the name. It was your father's own fault; how could he think to blackmail a good and honourable man, guilty merely of making the occasional mistake, into a marriage that would lead only to ruin? The same draught that killed Violet also took your father. It has served me well. There were no signs, and he was elderly and somewhat frail. His death was sudden but not unexpected.'

The driver of the trap appeared into the shocked silence. 'I have your trunk, miss. Is there anything else?'

'No, I will carry my bag myself.' She walked out to the open door. The driver handed her up and began to secure the trunk with a leather strap.

'Wait.' Hannah found her voice at last. 'Miss Hoyle, Sir George is dead.'

Miss Hoyle shook her head. She was still smiling. 'I do not believe you. You are lying; attempting to seek a petty revenge upon me after all I have told you. But it was time you heard the truth, was it not? You will have to sell this house and leave this area of Yorkshire now so you may do no more harm.'

Woodward said, imbuing his voice with a stern authority, 'Sir George was arrested by Sir Joseph Steading for the killing of Lavinia. He broke away from the escort, seized my horse and attempted to make his escape over the drop of the Cliff. It was a reckless action, doomed to failure.'

For a long, still moment, no one moved or spoke. Then at last Miss Hoyle gave a long, deep wail. 'No!' Before they could stop her, she had seized the reins, whipped up the horse and the trap was setting off, not along the drive to the road but bouncing and swaying along the path.

Hannah cried, 'She will overturn!'

Woodward gave chase, followed by the driver, but already the trap was gathering speed and it was obvious they could not reach her on foot.

And Hannah suddenly knew with a dreadful certainty where Miss Hoyle was going and what she would do. 'Wait,' she called as Woodward stopped. 'We can go left and cut her off.'

Woodward frowned. 'Does that go to the hall? I thought it the way to the doctor's house.'

Hannah was panting as they set off. 'Eventually, yes. But before that, it goes to the Cliff.'

'I see. And you think . . . ? Of course.'

'Don't wait for me. Go!'

Woodward nodded and set off, with Hannah doing her best to keep up as well as she was able. Although impeded by her skirts, she kept him in sight, her heart pounding relentlessly. And if she was wrong? If anything, she hoped she was. In that case, Miss Hoyle would be driving to the hall to see Lady Foxcroft.

Ahead of Woodward, the trap had now come into view, still being driven wildly and erratically, How it had not turned over, Hannah could not imagine. Mr Woodward had seen it too, for he was calling to Miss Hoyle.

Hannah could not hear what he was saying as the words floated upon the frosty air. Perhaps his presence distracted Miss Hoyle from her wild flight, or she may at last have hit a stone; for as Hannah gasped, the trap lurched and bumped and Miss Hoyle was thrown out.

Woodward ran towards her, but she was struggling to her feet and running onwards towards the Cliff. And as they both watched, she came to almost the exact spot where Sir George had met his end but a short time before — and leapt out, to be joined with her dear boy forever.

16

Hannah walked out from her one-time school to the nearest slope. She had spent several frantic days sending messages to the parents and guardians of her pupils; and when there was no immediate reply, going to see them herself, assuring them that all danger was past and the safety of their daughters could be guaranteed. She was telling the truth; even Lady Foxcroft had now been taken into custody, with Sir Joseph convinced she and Miss Hoyle had collaborated in a long-considered and evil plan.

The response had been the same wherever she went. Some were sympathetic and regretful, others angry and critical, but the results were the same. 'We are so sorry,' Mary Grey's mother had said, 'but you see, after all that has happened, we cannot even think of it.'

'I know the most dreadful things happened. But now everything is over.'

'All the same; it horrifies us that Mary was never safe from a monster such as Sir George turned out to be. And worse, that you could see fit to employ someone such as Miss Hoyle.'

Hannah had bowed her head. 'I only thought to do her a kindness.'

'We are sorry.' She had been shown out, politely but firmly.

Now Hannah turned and looked back at the house. This was the end of it. She had tried so hard to keep hold of the family inheritance, for Margaret's sake as much as her own — and lost.

She sensed a movement behind her as Mr Woodward approached. She looked away, knowing there were tears in her eyes. She said simply, 'It is over. They will not come back. Not one.'

He took her hand. 'I am so sorry to hear that.'

'Do not be. My whole life has been spent here; all the happiness of our childhood. But this house holds bad memories too, even before the events of the past weeks.' She paused. 'It is time to move on.' Woodward was still holding her hand. A few days ago, in the midst of the worst of it, she had felt he was about to offer marriage to her. Had he done so merely because he could see the difficulty of her position? Because he felt sorry for her? That would not do.

He said, 'I have been waiting to speak to you.'

'I know.'

'I do not think you do. Not entirely. My situation is about to change. As you know, I have been with Sir Joseph a great deal lately when previously I had barely met him.' He smiled. 'To begin with, he wondered whether I might know anything of Sir George's wasted errand in going to see him on the day after Violet was murdered. I had to admit the false message came from myself.'

'From you? Why?'

'I felt that you and I would be better able to discover the truth left to ourselves, before Sir George arrived. At that time, I did not even fully trust the doctor. So I arranged for Sir George to be conveniently sidetracked. Unfortunately, Lady Foxcroft waylaid me.' He shook his head. 'Only to tell me a poisonous tale of how you were ridden with jealousy and disappointment and now would not leave her husband alone. I have to admit, she was most convincing. Temporarily, I didn't know what to believe. Also, any advantage gained by Sir George's initial absence was lost; I was late back and could be of no use to you.'

'Do not think that. This has all ended as it should, and with justice done.'

'It is kind of you to say so. But I failed you, to my endless regret.' He shook his head. 'However, Sir Joseph is also willing to overlook my mistakes. He feels this living cannot make sufficient use of my abilities. I am repeating his words, you understand.'

Hannah smiled. 'Of course. I do not doubt it.'

'I am moving to a living in Manchester where the work, although difficult, will be of the utmost worth and value.' His voice rose with enthusiasm. 'I am to found a Sunday school where the children who work in the mills can begin to receive the first rudiments of an education.'

She tried to share his enthusiasm. 'You are leaving?'

'I am. And Hannah, I am asking you to come with me, as my wife; although I know it would be a great change for you, Manchester being a smoky industrial city. Perhaps too much of a change.'

'No.' Her voice was quivering. 'I do not believe so. But please do not ask because you feel sorry for us, or even because you need a suitable helpmeet — although that would suit me very well, because I now know what it is to be usefully employed, and I have enjoyed working with the children.' An idea struck her. 'Perhaps Margaret and I could come and work in your school?'

He laughed. 'Hannah, no. That is not why I want this. I love you. I have from first meeting you, when I admired your determination in the face of adversity, and your compassion and your need to protect and provide for your sister. If you cannot return my feelings, I must learn to live with that. But please, Hannah, tell me you *can* return my love.'

'Oh, yes, of course I do. I want only to be with you, wherever you need to be.'

Mr Woodward kissed her, and she was weeping with joy as his lips closed on hers, conscious of nothing more until a short distance behind them Margaret called, 'You had better take him now, Hannah. Or I must if you will not.'

Hannah laughed into Woodward's eyes. 'Oh, yes. Yes. Of course I will take him.'

With a new love and a new life beginning, she knew now that happiness lay before them.

We do hope that you have enjoyed reading this large print book.

Did you know that all of our titles are available for purchase?

We publish a wide range of high quality large print books including:
Romances, Mysteries, Classics
General Fiction
Non Fiction and Westerns

Special interest titles available in large print are:
The Little Oxford Dictionary
Music Book, Song Book
Hymn Book, Service Book

Also available from us courtesy of Oxford University Press:
Young Readers' Dictionary
(large print edition)
Young Readers' Thesaurus
(large print edition)

For further information or a free brochure, please contact us at:
Ulverscroft Large Print Books Ltd.,
The Green, Bradgate Road, Anstey,
Leicester, LE7 7FU, England.
Tel: (00 44) **0116 236 4325**
Fax: (00 44) **0116 234 0205**

Other titles in the
Linford Romance Library:

A HEART'S WAGER

Heidi Sullivan

Eva Copperfield has lived a life of poverty in the squalid slums of New York — until a sudden inheritance gives her the chance of a new life as lady of the manor in the English countryside. Her journey from rags to riches is complicated by the mysterious Ben — who is either a lord or a charlatan! Eva has to navigate the Atlantic and her heart before she can find a home . . . and love. Wagers are being made. Who will win?

MALLORCAN MAGIC

Jill Barry

On the rebound from a broken engagement, romance is the last thing on Eira's mind as she treats herself to a holiday in Mallorca. But two chance encounters with handsome entrepreneur Danny Carpenter, followed by a job offer as his children's nanny, set her on an entirely unexpected path. Soon she must deal not only with the complicated issue of falling for her employer, but also of coming to his defence when he is arrested and taken into custody for a crime he is certainly innocent of committing . . .

CAN'T BUY ME LOVE

Jo Weeks

When Jane Duncan's beloved grand-mother died, she left Jane the cottage in the little Scottish village where she had spent so many happy hours as a child. Relieved to leave the city life behind, Jane soon moved in. Her grandparents had lovingly tended the neighbouring Shaws estate as housekeeper and head gardener for many years. But Shaws has just been sold to Connor Macaulay, a wealthy American busi-nessman whose plans could mean the end of everything Jane holds dear. Sparks fly when they meet . . .

THE SILVER LINING

Wendy Kremer

Lady Stratton and her daughter Julia are living in straitened circumstances near the de Vere estate. When Gareth de Vere crashes his phaeton outside their cottage, he mistakes Julia for the maid. Although their attraction to each other grows with further encounters, their different social standings make it a mismatch. And despite a plot to provoke Gareth's feelings by his dissolute cousin, Fenton, Julia knows there is no chance of overcoming their circumstances — she is destined to love in vain . . .